To Mary!
With all good wishes,
and a Happy Birthday.
Beatrice Warren

Nurse in the Clouds

NURSE IN THE CLOUDS

Beatrice Warren

AVALON BOOKS
THOMAS BOUREGY AND COMPANY, INC.
NEW YORK

PRINTED IN THE UNITED STATES OF AMERICA
BY HADDON CRAFTSMEN, SCRANTON, PENNSYLVANIA

To my dear friend, Barbara Shumaker,
with love and appreciation

Chapter I

Listening once again to the heartbeat of the patient with an oxygen mask strapped to his face, Tracy Nichols, nurse practitioner at the Centerville Community Health Clinic, seemed concerned. Then she breathed a sigh of relief. For the helicopter from Kingsley had arrived! She could hear the throbbing of its engine and knew it would drop out of the sky and land on the field directly in front of the clinic.

She leaned over the patient. "The helicopter is here. You'll be on your way to San Francisco in a matter of minutes."

The patient opened his eyes and nodded. He had been brought to the health clinic by his wife, obviously in distress. The clutching pain in his chest and the difficulty in breathing had been classical symptoms of a heart attack. Tracy had started oxygen and administered needed medication before determining where to send him for coronary care. He had solved the problem by requesting transportation by helicopter to the veterans' hospital in San Francisco.

1

"My husband served in the army for over twenty years," his wife explained. "When he retired, we moved here to Northern California because of the rustic lifestyle and because we like the redwoods. It's so peaceful and quiet!"

She placed a hand on Tracy's arm. "My dear, how grateful I am for this modern clinic which, I realize, we have because of your efforts. I shudder to think what would have been the outcome if I had been forced to drive Marv all the way to Kingsley."

"Not my efforts alone. Dr. Sampson worked as hard to get the clinic as I did."

"Even so it is a major achievement for you. You have done a great service to the community."

Tracy, too, was proud of their achievement. She and Dr. Sampson—Dr. Clifford L. Sampson, to be exact—had seen the need for a clinic in this rural community and had solicited community support in starting one in a vacant office. They had soon been able to apply for and receive federal funding to erect their present facility.

She patted the patient's shoulder in reassurance. "It's a beautiful, clear day. You'll have a good flight to the hospital."

Tracy called members of the staff to help her. And by the time the helicopter touched ground, they had wheeled the patient outside, ready for immediate transfer. The paramedic climbed out of the still gyrating machine. Tracy went to meet him.

"Hi, Tracy," he greeted her. "I hear we're flying a heart-attack patient to the vets' hospital in San Francisco."

"That's right. He's a retired army man."

"How bad is he?" the pilot asked.

"He had a bad jolt. However, he seems stable enough to be moved."

"Has the doctor seen him?" the pilot asked.

"No. Dr. Sampson isn't in today."

"What about someone else? I'd feel easier if he had a doctor check him."

"Then you should have brought one from Kingsley!"

Just who did this redheaded pilot think he was? Tracy fumed to herself. She had seen enough heart patients to know what had to be done in an emergency.

"Tracy's as good as any doctor," the paramedic assured the pilot. "You can trust her judgment."

The pilot shrugged. "If you say so."

The patient was transferred to a stretcher and positioned in the helicopter. The paramedic took his place beside the patient. Within minutes the whirlybird lifted vertically into the air.

Eyes shaded, Tracy watched its steady climb. A small white object plummeted to the ground at her feet. She picked it up. It was a miniature parachute with a note attached.

"Green Eyes, I'll phone soon. We have a dinner date."

Tracy stared from the note to the helicopter, now a dot against a clear blue heaven. A smile played around her lips. What an audacious fellow that helicopter pilot was! Like Kevin. Except Kevin's eyes had been blue and his hair blond, while the helicopter pilot had red hair and dancing brown eyes. She had begged Kevin not to make the flight to Alaska even though his two passengers, ardent hunters, had offered to pay a handsome fee. They had been caught in an unexpected storm and the plane, a four-passenger Cessna, had crashed. There were no survivors.

Tracy had been devastated. Maybe she wouldn't have been so devastated if her father, a test pilot for the Air Force, hadn't been killed when a plane he was testing crashed. Anyway, there would be no dinner date with—Tracy stopped in mid-thought. She didn't even know the helicopter pilot's name. He must be the new owner of the helicopter service. Not that being the owner made any difference. She had vowed never again to become emotionally involved with a pilot.

That vow didn't extend to doctors. Tracy

had been an admirer of Dr. Clifford Sampson for four years. Her secret desire was that their working partnership would develop into marriage and a lifetime partnership. The main drawback to such a partnership was the incompatibility of their future goals. Tracy enjoyed the rural life, while Cliff yearned for city lights. Before his contract with the Centerville Community Health Clinic expired, he planned on finding a more lucrative urban practice.

Tracy's last patient of the day was a mother with a three-month-old baby. As a family nurse practitioner, Tracy had been trained in primary health care and had seen the mother regularly for prenatal visits, although she had gone to the hospital for delivery. Now Tracy would do routine checkups on the baby and advise the mother on proper health care.

With the baby on the scales, Tracy said to the mother, "Carmen has lost a pound. I think we had better start supplementing the breast feedings."

"Maybe that's why Carmen cries. You will tell me what to feed her?"

By the time the mother and baby left, the others had gone home and Tracy was left to lock up. As she walked to her car, she glanced up, wondering if the helicopter had returned and how Mr. Jackson had stood the trip.

Would the pilot really phone and invite her to have dinner with him? Green Eyes, he had called her. Well, she did have green eyes.

She drove the four miles home, smiling in satisfaction as she turned off the highway onto a graveled road. Then she drove a short distance before turning onto a lane leading to a weathered redwood cabin. How she and Cliff had argued when she bought the five-acre rancho!

"You're being foolish," he told her, "going into debt and tying yourself down. Besides, you're a woman alone. You know you can't keep that place up. You'll grow to hate it."

"But, Cliff," she had said, "I've always wanted a home in the country where I can have a horse. You weren't an Air Force brat. You don't know what it's like to have to move every two or three years. Owning my own home will be a dream come true."

"But five acres!"

"It's mostly wooded. Besides, this isn't Newport Beach. Land costs are much less here. And I'll have room to keep a horse and have a garden."

She really had gotten a bargain. An elderly retired couple had bought the land several years ago and had the cabin built. The long, wet winters and illness had sent them back to the Bay Area. Tracy had been good to them, going out of her way to help. In gratitude they had sold her the place, assuming the loan and with payments low enough for her to manage.

As she got out of her car, a sleek pinto horse neighed a welcome. She went to the fence and let the horse nuzzle her.

"I'm glad to see you, too," she said. "Let me change my clothes and we'll go for a nice long ride."

A primary reason for buying into the Rancho Hermosa Estates had been the horse trails which wound through the low hills. Tracy loved riding to the top of a ridge and watching the sunset. Occasionally Cliff borrowed a horse and rode with her. Each time he did this, she prayed that he would change his mind and decide to remain in Centerville. She still hadn't given up hope.

She returned from an hour's ride with glowing eyes and tingling blood. How could anyone ask for a better life? Even though salaries were low, and the hours at work long, she wouldn't change her job for the best job in the biggest hospital in all of California!

Returning to the lean-to stable, Tracy fed the pinto a bucket of oats and barley, and made sure the water trough was filled before leaving her for the night. Walking toward the redwood cabin with its solar windows and captain's walk, she smiled in satisfaction. She entered through the back door, pausing to glance around the living room and open kitchen, then went up the stairs to her bedroom. She took a hot shower and slipped into a comfortable housecoat, then went downstairs to quickly eat some dinner.

Tracy had poured herself a glass of lemonade when the phone rang.

"Green Eyes? This is Andy Carlton. We delivered the heart patient safely to the vets' hospital. He stood the trip very well. The doctors seem confident he'll recover."

"Why, thank you! It's very thoughtful of you to let me know how well he's doing."

"Oh, I have an ulterior motive! It gives me an excuse to phone. Did you get my message?"

"You mean the one you dropped from the helicopter?"

"Yes. How about dinner tomorrow? My calendar is clear. Of course, something could come up, but that's a fact of life for a helicopter operator. I grab my chances when they come."

Tracy wondered at the way her heart behaved. Why was it beating so erratically? This wasn't Kevin. This was Andy Carlton, a man she had seen for the first time today, and then for a mere five minutes. Even in that short space of time his audacious manner had irritated her. Of course, she wouldn't go to dinner with him!

"I'm sorry, but I can't go to dinner with you tomorrow. I have another engagement."

"Something you can wiggle out of? I might not have another free evening for two weeks."

Tracy hesitated. She didn't have a confirmed date. She just made a habit of keeping Friday evening free in case Cliff wanted to do something. He was out of the valley until Sunday. She could look forward to a lonely weekend. Unless...

"Are you sure you want to drive twenty-five miles just to take me out to dinner?"

"Would I call and ask you if I didn't? I would even drive another twenty-five miles to Mendocino. If that's where you want to go. I'd settle for the Centerville Hotel. I hear they've done an authentic restoration and that the food is pretty good."

"The food is excellent. Joe and Betty deserve all the praise they're getting."

"Then that means you'll go to dinner with me?"

How could she say no? Tracy capitulated.

"What time will you be by for me?"

"How about seven? I have some work to do here at the office and probably won't get away any earlier."

"Seven sounds good. I often get tied up at the clinic and have to stay late."

"By the way, how do I find you?"

After giving Andy detailed directions, Tracy took her glass of lemonade and went out on the balcony. She stood by the rail gazing through the tall redwoods to the azure sky where a lone star peeked down at her.

Smiling at her childishness, she thought of making a wish.

But what would she wish? That Cliff would decide to remain here in Centerville? Maybe it would be better to wish she could meet someone who shared her interests. She felt sure that wouldn't be Andy Carlton.

Feeling chilly, Tracy went back inside. By ten o'clock she was ready for bed. It had been a long day and six o'clock came far too soon.

On Friday, even though Tracy had patients enough to keep her busy, her mind wandered to the evening. She had to admit to a feeling of excitement. There was something about the helicopter pilot—a kind of daring, exciting aura. Had he learned his helicoptering in the army or navy? Frankly, Tracy thought, he seemed young to own his own company. Maybe his youthful appearance was deceiving.

She had seen her last patient and had congratulated herself on being able to leave a few minutes early when the foreman from the sawmill phoned to say he was bringing in a man with a badly cut hand. He had accidentally touched one of the operating saws.

With a resigned sigh, Tracy set up a suture tray and was ready and waiting when the man arrived. It proved to be rather a nasty cut. But since no tendons were involved, Tracy sutured it herself. She dressed the wound, gave him a tetanus shot, and advised him to return on Monday. By the time she drove home, it was after six o'clock. She would have to rush in order to be ready when Andy arrived.

The phone rang while Tracy was in the shower. She grabbed a towel to wrap around herself, then hurried to answer it.

"Is this Tracy Nichols?" a woman's voice asked.

"Yes."

"This is Sylvia Duncan, Andrew Carlton's partner."

Tracy's heart took a nose dive. Andy had crashed! Just like Kevin and her father! His helicopter had gone down!

"Andy asked me to call. He tried to reach you before he took off, but you weren't available."

"Is—is something wrong?" Tracy managed to ask.

"The usual thing, especially when he has a date." Tracy detected a note of bitterness in the voice. "He's off on an emergency flight. A logger was crushed beneath a falling tree. He said to tell you he should be back by seven.

However, I wouldn't count on it if I were you. He'll phone you when he gets back."

As Tracy replaced the phone, a shiver set her teeth to chattering. She couldn't go through another air tragedy. When Andy called, she would tell him she wouldn't go to dinner. Not tonight or any other night. She hardly knew him and look how uptight she was. No matter how persuasive he was or how much charm Mr. Andrew Carlton turned on, she would not give in.

Never again would she go through the agony of wondering when someone she cared about might crash and be killed. Before doing that, she would sell her rancho, give up her horse, and move back to the city with Cliff.

Chapter II

Eight o'clock came and still no call from Andy. Tracy assured herself it was better this way. If Andy didn't phone, she wouldn't be tempted to change her mind. With no television, she put a record, a Mozart piano concerto, on the stereo and tried to relax with a book. Her eyes kept straying to the clock. Had something happened? Andy should have returned before this unless something had gone wrong.

She had decided to fix herself something to eat when a car pulled up outside. Tracy hurried to the window. Andy! Thank heaven nothing had happened to him. Filled with relief, she went to meet him. He had stopped and was gazing around, a look of wry amusement on his face.

"This is quite a layout you have here," he told her. "You can't live here all by yourself!"

"I not only can, I do live here by myself."

"But it's so isolated!"

"Not really. I have neighbors less than a mile away. Then my horse. And deer come to

13

graze—that's why the high fence. To keep them out of my garden."

He slipped an arm around her and, laughing, bent to kiss her.

"Green Eyes, you amaze me!" He held her away, his gaze moving from her ankles to her face. "You don't strike me as the rural type. You would look more at home in a luxurious apartment in San Francisco."

Face flushed, green eyes flashing, Tracy pulled free of his hold.

"For your information, I left the city because I wanted to live in the country. Being here is my choice."

Dryly Andy said, "I take it there's been opposition. Say, your family—or boyfriend?"

Tracy shrugged. "Some opposition, yes. My mother can't understand why I moved up here, away from her and my stepfather. Mom's perfectly happy in a luxurious apartment in Los Angeles."

As they entered the house and Andy's sharp gaze took in the faded sofa, scuffed end tables, unmatched chairs, and scattered throw rugs, Tracy again became defensive.

"I wanted a house and a horse more than furniture. These are mostly Mom's discards."

"This looks great. You should see where I'm living. In a room behind my office." Again the wry smile. "Have you priced helicopters lately?"

Caught unawares, Tracy looked startled, then laughed.

"I can't say that I have. Horses are more my speed."

"Some people consider the helicopter the workhorse of the air. A helicopter may not be as glamorous as fancier planes, but it does jobs nothing else can do."

"How did you get interested in helicopters?" Tracy asked.

"In the army. There I saw what they could do."

"Oh? My father was an Air Force pilot."

"Was?"

"Yes. He was killed while on a test flight of a new airplane."

"I say, that's too bad!" Andy glanced at his watch. "I don't know about you, but I'm ready to eat. Will the hotel still be open, or are we too late?"

"I keep a good supply of food. If you'll settle for lamb chops and a green salad, we can eat right here."

"That sounds great. In fact, I'm a good salad maker. I'll volunteer for that job."

"Do you want the lamb chops barbecued on the grill, or broiled in the oven?"

"Barbecued, by all means. Show me where things are and I'll start the fire."

As Tracy flew about getting things together, she fairly bubbled with happiness.

Cliff never offered to help in the kitchen. Or even to barbecue. When he came to dinner, she tried to have everything ready for him. What fun it was to have someone to work along with her.

In fact, dangerously pleasant fun. She must not let this happen too often. Next time she would insist on going out to dinner.

In June the evenings were too cool to eat outside. Tracy got out her china, a set her mother had bought her in Japan, and her new wine goblets, made by a local artist.

As they sat down to eat, Tracy felt Andy's ardent gaze. He raised his wineglass.

"To us! May this be the first of many such occasions."

Hand trembling, Tracy picked up her glass and put it to her lips. However, she put it down without drinking. The knowledge that Andy had been on an emergency flight and the long agonizing wait for his phone call had given her a sample of what she would endure should she let herself become emotionally involved. No, evenings like this could not become a habit!

"Tell me," Andy said as he cut into a succulent lamb chop, "exactly how you got to Centerville from Los Angeles. This is such a remote area I didn't think anyone ever heard about it. At least not that far south."

"I doubt if many people have. Mendocino,

yes. Centerville, no. My coming here is rather a long story."

Brown eyes dancing, Andy said, "I've got all night. No calls until noon tomorrow."

Tracy gazed at him, taking in his shock of red hair, snub nose, upturned mouth, and determined chin, all dominated by his lively brown eyes. As relaxed as he seemed, there was still that aura of daring and bravado. Mr. Andrew Carlton could be a very exciting person to associate with.

"As I told you, Dad was in the Air Force. For the first twelve years of my life we moved on the average of every two to three years. Two things I wanted most were a flower garden and a horse. Dad kept telling me that the very next move would be to a place where I could have both my flower garden and a horse. Of course, that never happened. Then when Dad was killed—well, Mom likes the city. Actually, we lived on the edge of Beverly Hills. Mom loves all the shops and restaurants. I'd already made up my mind to be a nurse. After I graduated, I heard about a program where a nurse could get advanced training as a nurse practitioner by agreeing to work in a rural area with a shortage of medical facilities. So here I am!"

"Then you really like it here?"

"Yes. It's a totally different lifestyle. I'm happier here than I've ever been." Tracy took a sip of wine, then asked, "How did you get to this part of California?"

"Expediency. I knew I didn't want to make the army my career, but I did want to continue flying helicopters. Looking around, this seemed to be the best location. The owner of the helicopter service in Kingsley wanted to sell. So far things are working out fairly well."

"Isn't it dangerous?"

"Dangerous? Helicopters?" Andy looked puzzled. "Just what do you mean?"

"Isn't there the danger of crashing and being killed?"

"Helicopters rarely have fatal accidents. Because of their slow speed and maneuverability, they're not as vulnerable as other aircraft."

"The woman who phoned me, is she really your partner?"

"Sylvia?" Did she detect a note of caution? Tracy wondered. "Yes, Sylvia is my partner. Financially, that is. Her husband, Jim, was a buddy of mine in the army. We had planned on going in business together. Then, in one of those freak accidents, his helicopter crashed and he was killed."

"But you told me how safe helicopters were!"

"They're a lot safer than most other aircraft, but that doesn't mean they're infallible.

It just seldom happens, that's all. Anyway,
Sylvia wanted in with me. She insisted Jim
would want her to use his insurance money
that way."

"What exactly do you do besides air ambulance service?"

"Oh, a variety of things. We offer a charter
service, frost control, timber cruising, lifting,
and aerial and cinema photography."

"I've met one of your pilots, Tim O'Hara.
Are there any others?"

"Not right now. Tim and I manage all the
flights so far. When we can wrangle another
helicopter, we'll need another pilot. Maybe
two. Then we could have a little time off."

They took their coffee to the living room.
Sitting on the sofa, Andy's arm strayed
around Tracy's shoulders. When she inched
away, his knowing grin unnerved her. He
stood up, took her hands, and pulled her to
her feet. His arms went around her, and his
lips found hers. She stiffened in his arms.

With a wry smile, he released her. "Time
for me to head back over the hill. It's been a
great evening."

Tracy watched him drive away, totally con-
fused by her emotions. He hadn't said he
would call or see her again. But did she want
him to call? Did she want to see him again?
Of course, helicopters crashed! She must put
Andy out of her life!

ɔ

Besides, she loved Cliff. What she really wanted was for the two of them to continue working together as they had done for the past four years. When it came to actually leaving, she would stake her future on Cliff not being able to give up all they had accomplished here.

With Cliff out of the valley, Tracy looked forward to a weekend in which to indulge her two favorite pastimes—riding Molly, her pinto mare, and working in her flower garden.

On Saturday she dressed in faded jeans and T-shirt, ate her breakfast, then went outside.

One look and she cried out in dismay. Deer had gotten into her garden! Now all that remained were bare stems. She knelt down, tears in her eyes. All her work! All for nothing. But how had a deer gotten in? Could one have jumped over the fence?

She got up to check the fence and noticed the gate unlatched and swinging open. Andy. He had not shut the gate and she hadn't gone out to check it.

Heartsick and discouraged, Tracy wandered back into the house. How could Andy have been so careless? Cliff would never have left the gate unlatched. He knew how much her garden meant to her.

Should she call Andy and tell him what

had happened? What good would it do? The plants were destroyed. She would simply have to be sure he closed the gate next time he came. Next time—he hadn't said anything about a next time. Maybe if she called...

Andy answered the phone himself.

"Oh, Tracy. I haven't got but a minute. I'm picking a couple up in Mendocino and flying them to San Francisco to the airport. Can I call you back?"

Feeling rebuffed by his brisk voice, Tracy blurted, "You left my gate open and the deer destroyed my garden."

"That's too bad, but I can't do anything about it now. I've got to be on my way."

What a heartless beast, Tracy fumed when the line went dead. He hadn't even said he was sorry! But what would a garden mean to him? All he cared about was his precious helicopter business.

Turning her back on her garden, she used her pent-up energy in cleaning house. By four o'clock she had everything in shining order, so she saddled Molly for a ride. Galloping along the trail, the wind tousling her shiny brown hair, her eyes glowing, she forgot everything but the thrill of the moment. She returned two hours later and found Cliff sitting on the deck waiting for her.

"What in the world are you doing here?"

Tracy asked, sliding off the horse and gazing at Cliff. "I thought you weren't due back until tomorrow."

"I finished my business and remembered we were invited to the wine tasting and barbecue at the Spencer Valley Winery. I promised Maurice we would be there."

"That is tonight! I had forgotten."

"We're due there now. How soon can you be ready?"

"Give me ten minutes to bed Molly down for the night and twenty to shower and dress. They certainly won't eat before seven." Turning Molly, she added, "Have some lemonade from the fridge. I won't be long."

Tracy soon hurried upstairs, pleased that Cliff had remembered the barbecue. She showered, dressed in an off-white pants outfit, ran a comb through her hair, and applied a bit of lipstick. Grabbing her purse, she ran back downstairs.

"That was quick," Cliff greeted her. "And you look great." He kissed her. "I missed you."

Returning his kiss, Tracy said, "And I missed you. Things don't seem the same when you're gone."

"But you manage very well." As they started down the path toward the gate, Cliff stopped, his gaze on Tracy's ruined flower garden. "I say, what happened? Just look at this!"

"I know. A deer got in the yard last night."

"You mean, one actually jumped the fence?"

"No. The gate was left open."

As they turned off on the highway, Cliff asked, "Did you have any serious cases while I was gone?"

"One heart attack. A retired army man. We had to fly him by helicopter to the veterans' hospital in San Francisco."

Saying this brought the redheaded helicopter pilot to mind. He must be back from his flight to San Francisco by now. What if he phoned this evening? But, of course, Tracy had no reason to expect to hear from him. And it might be weeks before another patient would require air ambulance service.

Anyway, Cliff had come back early to attend the barbecue at the Spencer Valley Winery. He liked it here, too. Of course, he wouldn't leave. Things would work out the way she wanted. They would be married and continue working together just as they were doing now.

Chapter III

The winery, rustic redwood with windows overlooking a hillside vineyard, was located in the heart of Spencer Valley. Tracy never drove by without admiring the bright flower beds.

For the barbecue, tables had been set up under an arbor. When Cliff and Tracy arrived, they were met by the savory odor of braising meat.

The owner hurried to meet them. "Cliff! Tracy! I'm delighted that you came. I had given up seeing you here today."

"We almost didn't make it," Tracy said. "Cliff came back from San Francisco especially to be here."

"Then I'm doubly honored! Come, meet our other guests."

Their host led them toward a group clustered around a sultry blonde with alluring blue eyes. Tracy and Cliff recognized and greeted everyone in the group but the blonde. The winery owner introduced them.

"Sylvia, I'd like you to meet Dr. Sampson

and Tracy Nichols. We owe our fine medical clinic to their efforts."

The blonde's eyes narrowed as she turned her full gaze on Tracy.

"Tracy Nichols. We've talked on the phone, I believe. It is nice to meet you in person."

"Oh, you must be Andrew Carlton's partner!"

At that moment, Andy appeared at the entrance to the arbor. Tracy felt his gaze and turned. His face all smiles, Andy came to her side.

"Tracy, this is a surprise! I'm delighted to see you."

The blonde took a possessive hold on his arm. "Tracy is here with Dr. Sampson," she said. "Have you met him?"

Andy held out his hand to Cliff. "No, I haven't had the honor. I've heard about your work at the Centerville Community Health Clinic, however. I picked my first patient up there the other day."

"That was Marvin Jackson, wasn't it?" the winery owner asked. "He was supposed to be here with us today. It's too bad about his heart attack."

"He stood the helicopter ride very well," Andy said. He turned to Tracy. "Have you heard anything more on his condition?"

"No. Just what you told me."

Their host moved them on to a table with

an impressive array of wines. They each took
small samples of wine and moved to a table
spread with appetizers.

"Ummm! Try this crab dip!" Tracy urged
Cliff.

"Maurice has a nice setup here," Cliff said
after agreeing with Tracy about the crab dip.
"He's done well in the few years we've been
in Spencer Valley."

Smiling in remembrance, Tracy nodded.
"His daughter was one of our first patients at
the clinic. Remember how she fell and broke
her arm? The X-ray equipment had just been
installed and we were so proud!"

"Yes, it seemed an achievement at the
time. But things move so slow around here.
One of my meetings was at U.C. Hospital.
There's excitement, a feeling of urgency
there. New concepts of medicine crop up
every day."

Tracy looked at Cliff in dismay. "But look
how badly we're needed here! How grateful
our patients are."

"And how routine our days! Colds, sore
throats, an occasional auto accident—routine stuff mostly."

"That's what family medicine is all about.
That and preventive medicine. Don't you
think it's important to help people stay well?"

"Of course, it is. Only—"

"Dr. Cliff, you're just the person I've been

looking for!" a plump, middle-aged woman with a firm mouth and light-blue eyes interrupted. "I'd like you to meet my brother, Dr. James Andrews, from North Dakota. He has a rural practice and wants to know more about our clinic."

Tracy, not being included in the introduction, wandered away, smiling wryly. Ever since she and Mrs. Bentley, a member of the Centerville Community Health Clinic Board, had disagreed over an item or two related to clinic policy—Mrs. Bentley wanted nicer furniture in the waiting room—the older woman had ignored her.

Tracy let her gaze move from Andy to Cliff. How different they were, both in looks and temperament. Cliff, with his dark hair and elegant beard, reminded her of a portrait she had once seen of a turn-of-the-century dandy. His deep brown eyes showed compassion, yet could be firm and uncompromising when necessary. He would be considered very handsome by most women, but not with the dashing, heart-throbbing good looks of the redheaded helicopter pilot.

Rather than join one of the scattered groups, all deep in animated conversation, Tracy wandered along a path leading to a vineyard.

"There's a tranquility here that I love," a voice said at her side.

"Andy!" Tracy gasped. "How you startled me."

"I didn't mean to startle you. You looked so pensive. A penny for your thoughts."

"My thoughts are your thoughts. I, too, love the tranquility here. Often I gaze out over the valley and try to picture it as it was when the first settlers came here. Can you imagine what they would have thought if a helicopter had landed in one of their fields?"

Andy chuckled. "They would have thought some alien from another planet had landed!" Musingly he added, "I can remember the first time I saw a helicopter. It reminded me of a giant insect. The last thing I expected to become was a helicopter pilot."

"I've known since I was six years old that I wanted to live in the country and have my own horse. A horse and a flower garden."

"I'm sorry about your garden. Did the deer do much damage?"

"Indeed they did! There isn't a single leaf left. I'm going to have to completely replant."

"What can I do to make it up to you?"

"If you're good with a shovel, you can help me spade the area."

"No shoveling. I'm sorry. How about letting me take you to dinner instead?"

"That won't replace my garden. But speaking of dinner, I see people sitting down at the tables. Cliff will be looking for me."

"I guess we had better amble back," Andy said.

They were met by a furious Sylvia. Tracy moved off to find Cliff, aware that if looks were daggers, she would have one between her shoulders. So, she thought, Sylvia Duncan aspires to being more than a financial partner at Carlton Helicopters. She wants to be Mrs. Andrew Carlton.

The steaks, seasoned and cooked to perfection, were accompanied by a variety of salads, garlic bread, and a wide choice of wines. Their host, Maurice Benoit, and his wife, Annette, circulated among the tables seeing most graciously to the needs of their guests.

"Maurice and Annette deserve to succeed," Cliff observed. "They have worked hard, and they have excellent wines. I suppose now it's a matter of marketing."

"I hear that two more wineries are soon to open tasting rooms here in Spencer Valley. Competition is keen," someone said.

"And that means more patients at the clinic. Our case load could easily double," Cliff said.

Tracy fervently hoped so. Then maybe Cliff would be content to remain here.

Because of the distances many of the guests had to drive, the festivities broke up early. Andy came to say good-by.

"I don't know my schedule for next week yet, but I'll be in touch. Just keep some time open."

"My schedule is full. I can't promise anything," Tracy said.

"Oh?" Andy's arch grin infuriated her. "You're not still mad because I left the gate open, are you?"

"What's this about an open gate?" Cliff asked, appearing at Tracy's side.

"When I left Tracy's last night, I neglected to close the gate."

"So that's how the deer got in!" Cliff said. "That does you in! In Tracy's book, a criminal offense. Her garden and her horse are the two main interests in her life."

Sylvia tugged at Andy's arm. "It's getting late. I'm ready to leave." Her frosty gaze brushed Tracy. "Andy really is very busy. Maintaining a helicopter service leaves little time for social activities. I'm sure you understand."

Tracy, her lips tilted in a half smile, nodded. She understood all too well. Sylvia Duncan wanted an open field, without competition. Apparently Andy wasn't as cooperative as she would like him to be.

Driving home, Cliff said, "What's this about Andy leaving the gate open? What was he doing at your place?"

Tracy darted a questioning glance at Cliff.

Would it matter to him if another man became interested in her?

"Andy was piloting the helicopter that transported Mr. Jackson to San Francisco." She shrugged. "He invited me to have dinner with him, then got delayed. We had planned on having dinner at the Centerville Hotel, but it was so late we ate at home instead. I guess it really was my fault about the gate. I should have gone out to make sure it was closed."

"What time was it when he left?"

Tracy's temper flared. "What business is it of yours? I don't need a keeper!"

"I don't know about that. There's something about that helicopter pilot—I'm not sure I trust him."

Surprised, Tracy said, "Not trust Andy? Why, he's an excellent pilot. I'd certainly trust him with any patient I wanted sent by helicopter."

"I wasn't referring to his ability as a pilot. It's where women are concerned that I don't trust him."

Tracy glanced at Cliff. Then he was jealous! Maybe she could add a little fuel to the flame.

"He certainly is fascinating. So dashing. I think of him as a commando, someone eager to perform daring exploits."

Cliff snorted, "I'd call it being reckless.

Pure bravado. A very unstable character."

At least that couldn't be said of Cliff, Tracy told herself. He was steady, firm of character, and steadfast, all admirable traits, especially in a doctor. Yet even he yearned for a more exciting practice. And a more lucrative one. Apparently there wasn't the challenge here, now that they had an established medical facility, that he craved. Was she being fair in wanting him to remain here?

"How about coming to dinner tomorrow?" Tracy asked as Cliff started back to his car after seeing her to the house.

"I can't. I'm having dinner with the Bentleys." He bent down and kissed Tracy on her nose. "If you would mend your fences, you'd be socially acceptable at the Bentleys' and would be going with me."

"Why should I apologize? I was right, you know that. We don't need fancy drapes and an expensive couch in the waiting room. I can get along very well without going to the Bentleys' to dinner."

"I know. However, it would make for better relations on the clinic board. There may come a time when you'll need her support. She does have a certain amount of prestige and power, you realize that."

"Oh, fiddle! Our differences weren't that great. She can't stand not having everything go her way. I'm not caving in just to appease her."

"You're as stubborn as she is. I hope you won't regret it." Tracy heard the gate click. "Good night. I'll see you on Monday."

Tracy spent Sunday morning pulling out the ruined plants and preparing the ground for new seeds. She would have to get them tomorrow. Anyway, it would be a few days before she would have the time to replant.

She spent a half hour grooming Molly, but decided against going for a ride until later in the day. Tracy kept one ear alert for the telephone. Andy just might call even though she hadn't encouraged him. Nor had she agreed to go to dinner. Besides, Sylvia would see to it that he was kept well occupied. Tracy would do well to blot Mr. Andrew Carlton out of her thoughts.

She thought she had succeeded until, on Monday, she heard the unmistakable sound of a helicopter and looked out the window. It was landing here! Why? Cliff came out of his office.

"Did we get word that they were bringing a patient by helicopter?" he asked.

"Of course not, or I would have told you," Tracy assured him.

They went together out the emergency entrance. The helicopter door opened and Andy jumped out. He waved a package at Tracy. She looked questioningly at Cliff, then hurried across the driveway.

"Here's seeds to replant your garden,"

Andy said with his impudent grin. "I selected a wide variety."

Tracy accepted the seeds, glancing quickly through the packages.

"Andy, I'm not exactly going into the flower business! I could replant Golden Gate Park with what you have here."

"I wanted to make sure you had enough. I'm on my way to Eureka. Have a forestry job up there. I'll be in touch."

He climbed back into the helicopter, adjusted the controls, and, with a jaunty wave, lifted off the ground. Blown by the churned air, Tracy waved back. Andy leaned out and shouted something, but whatever he said was drowned out by the copter. Tracy walked slowly back to the clinic.

"What was that all about?" Cliff asked.

Tracy showed him the flower seeds. Cliff snorted.

"Sheer bravado. I warned you that he was unreliable and reckless."

"Oh, I don't know," Tracy replied, her face lit by an inner glow. "I thought it romantic!"

"Romantic or not, delivering seeds by helicopter, especially while he's establishing himself, was a waste of time and money. A reckless, grandiose gesture."

Smiling to herself, Tracy said nothing more but returned to her office. Cliff was undoubtedly right. It was a grandiose gesture.

But right for Andy. Besides, he hadn't really gone out of his way. What Tracy would have liked to know was whether or not Sylvia knew he had brought her flower seeds. She was willing to bet Andy had not shared this maneuver with his partner.

Chapter IV

Getting out of her car on Tuesday morning and gazing at the white-frame clinic, Tracy smiled in satisfaction.

She was still smiling as she entered the waiting room and said "Good morning" to Maria, the receptionist.

Cliff hadn't yet arrived, but Mrs. Connors, a gray-haired, pink-cheeked nurse with a clipped British accent, was checking supplies.

"Good morning, Hazel," Tracy greeted her. "Do we have a heavy schedule today?"

"Dr. Cliff certainly does after being away last Thursday and Friday. You know what happens!"

After putting her purse away, Tracy went back to the waiting room to look at the appointment book.

"I think half the babies in Spencer Valley will be in for a checkup today," Maria told her.

"I see a couple of prenatal visits, also. That should keep me busy."

There would no doubt be several unsched-
uled visits. Emergencies of some kind. A
baby with an earache, a child with a possible
fracture, not to mention the possibility of another heart attack or someone who had suffered a stroke. If only Cliff could realize that
serving the community in this way was vital
even if it wasn't very lucrative.

In the middle of the afternoon Cliff stopped
by Tracy's office.

"How about going to the movies tonight?"

"What's playing?"

"Some French film. Maurice and Annette
saw it in Kingsley. Said it was great."

"I'd like to go with you."

"I'll pick you up at seven. Unless you'd like
to go to dinner first."

"I'd better not. By the time I get home and
feed and exercise Molly, there won't be time."

Tracy had been pleased when the old Had-
ley barn had been turned into a movie house.
The films were selected and shown first in
Kingsley, passed on to Centerville, then on to
some other towns. As pleased as she had
been, however, this was only the third movie
she had attended.

"I don't know why we don't come more
often," Cliff remarked as, each with a con-
tainer of popcorn, he and Tracy settled into
their seats.

"I know," Tracy said. "It seems there's

always something to do. A class to attend, some function at the grange, not to mention weeding my garden."

"And riding Molly! Don't forget to mention that."

Chuckling, Tracy replied, "Oh, I won't! I'm considering riding in the horse show at the fair in September. Of course, I'd be a rank beginner. Some of those kids who have ridden since they were two—well, I wouldn't stand a chance beside them."

"Absolutely no! You're not to consider any such thing," Cliff stated in his most uncompromising tone of voice.

"And why not?" Tracy demanded.

"Because you've got all you can do without starting anything else. I told you not to burden yourself with that property and a horse. It will be worse when Molly has her colt. I can't imagine why you want to go through that."

"I think Molly deserves to be a mother, and I'm looking forward to having a colt to care for. I won't neglect my duties at the clinic. Molly doesn't really take that much time. Just feeding and watering."

"And grooming and riding, not to mention the task of finding someone to look after her when you want to go away."

"Which isn't very often. I'm happy at home."

"I know! Too much so. I'm not sure it's good for you. A person needs stimulating change. I'm thinking of getting tickets to the symphony in San Francisco for next season. I hope you'll go with me."

"That would mean being away overnight, wouldn't it? Frankly, I'd rather just go to the plays at Kingsley or Mendocino. Some of their productions are outstanding."

"But not on a par with San Francisco! I'm looking forward to moving closer to the city."

"Then you found an opening while you were away?"

"Not really. However, I have two good leads. Something will come from one of them. I'm sure of that."

The house went dark, the screen lit up, and music filled the air. Both Tracy and Cliff settled back in their seats, their attention on the movie screen.

The film, a light, funny French farce, kept them entertained and laughing. Cliff was still chuckling as they went to his car.

"I enjoyed that. I'll have to pay more attention to what's showing. Since they go to all the effort to get the movies, the least we can do is support their efforts."

Tracy looked at Cliff wondering if he was as discontented here in Spencer Valley as he said he was. If only she could be sure of how he felt! One minute she thought nothing would keep him here, and the next minute she felt nothing could tear him away. This kept her up one second, down the next. And Cliff called Andy unstable!

The rest of the week passed quietly and, to Tracy, quickly. It seemed no time at all until Friday. She suggested to Cliff that they spend the evening at her place and barbecue, but he said no. He wanted to drive to Kingsley and have dinner at a new restaurant.

They were sitting at a table, waiting for their food, when Tracy looked up and saw Sylvia standing in the doorway.

Cliff saw her, too. "Do you mind if I ask Sylvia Duncan to join us?" he asked.

"Of course not," Tracy assured him. Sylvia should have some information about Andy.

The striking blonde followed Cliff. At the table she paused, looking down at Tracy.

"Thank you for inviting me to your table. Andy was supposed to be here to meet someone. But his forestry job is taking extra time. Since he won't be back for another week or so, he phoned and asked me to do the honors." She looked around the room. "I don't see anyone that fits the description Andy gave me. Either he's late or won't show."

"What can I get you to drink?" Cliff asked, holding her chair while she sat down.

Sylvia glanced toward Tracy. "White wine will be fine," she said.

After giving the order to the waitress, Cliff said, "Isn't it rather strange for a woman to be involved in a helicopter business?"

"Not really," Sylvia replied. "My husband was a helicopter pilot and a friend of Andy's. They had planned to start up their own company. Or buy out a small company. I felt Jim would want me to carry on in his place. It meant a lot to him."

"Are you interested in flying a whirlybird?"

Sylvia shook her head. "Not since Jim crashed. I'm happy running the office. Someone has to answer the phone, schedule flights, do the bookkeeping, and a multitude of other tasks Andy doesn't have time to do."

"Such as keep his appointments?" Cliff suggested with a broad smile.

"That, too," Sylvia said. She frowned. "I really had expected him back today. We have an unusually heavy schedule for tomorrow. Tim will have to fly more hours than we like our pilots to be in the air."

"What's keeping Andy at Eureka longer than he planned?" Tracy asked.

"Unseasonal weather, for one thing. Then, too, the job turned out to involve more hours in the air than he had counted on. However, he's done other jobs for this lumber company and feels he has to stay until they complete the survey."

Just then a rather distraught bald-headed man entered and looked quickly around the room.

"There's Mr. Summers now!"

Excusing herself, Sylvia hurried over to the man hovering in the doorway.

"Sylvia is a beautiful, charming woman," Cliff remarked. "I suppose that helicopter pilot has her bewitched, too. I can't imagine any other reason for her isolating herself in a town like Kingsley! There's nothing to hold anyone here that I can see."

"Oh, Cliff! Kingsley is a very nice town. True, it's not Los Angeles or San Francisco, but the people who move here come because they want to get away from the city. They like life in the slow lane."

"Well, they can have it! Personally I can't wait to get back in the fast lane. Life here is too slow for my taste."

Yet there was an urgency in Cliff's good-night kiss that Tracy hadn't felt before.

"Don't you think it's time we made some decision about our future?" he asked. "About getting married."

"I—I—not tonight," Tracy hedged.

"It's that helicopter pilot, isn't it? You won't give me an answer because of him. I expected you to have more common sense than to fall for a show-off like him."

"I haven't fallen for him! I hardly know

him. Besides, you were quite taken by Sylvia Duncan!"

"All I said is that she is both charming and beautiful. Frankly, I can't imagine her sticking it out in Kingsley for very long. She's not the rural type."

"But her husband was in the armed forces. She must have lived in some pretty dreary places, following him. She may surprise you and really enjoy being here."

"We weren't talking about her. I wanted an answer from you. I have two serious possibilities for relocating in the Bay Area. I'm expecting you to go with me."

"Leave Centerville and the clinic? Cliff, I've put too much of myself into establishing medical care here to leave. Besides—how can I give up my rancho and my horse?"

"That's why I objected to you getting them. I have never seriously considered remaining here. You know that."

"But you seem happy here and you always enjoy what social activities there are."

"What social activities there are. That's the crux of it. There aren't many to my taste. And I want a more stimulating medical practice."

"We can't settle this tonight. Let me give it more thought."

Getting into her pajamas and robe, and brushing her teeth, she did manage to keep her thoughts on her relationship to Cliff. If she loved him enough to marry him, shouldn't she be eager to go with him even if it meant giving up all she had worked to achieve here in Centerville? She had been so sure that Cliff would not leave. Now that she knew differently, what was she going to do?

Sighing deeply, Tracy went to bed. If Cliff didn't change his mind, then what? Things were getting more complicated by the day. Last week her dreams weren't invaded by a daring, laughing-eyed, redheaded helicopter pilot. Even more disturbing was the fact that Andy's dream kisses affected her in a way Cliff's kisses never had.

She had dozed off when the phone rang. Sleepily, she reached for the receiver. What emergency needed her attention now?

"Green Eyes? I called earlier. You must have been out."

Wide awake now, Tracy said, "Andy! Where are you?"

"Still in Eureka. Wishing you were here with me. It's going to be a long weekend. I expected to be home before now, but the weather has been bad and there's more work than I realized."

"If you're not working, can't you fly home, then go back on Monday?"

"Oh, I'll be in the air tomorrow! Coming home for one day would be too costly. After every thousand hours of flight time, we have to do a complete overhaul. Would you believe it costs me forty dollars every time I start the engine?"

"No, but then I know nothing about helicopters."

"You'll learn. Anyway, what I called to say is that I'll be home on Friday. If I bring fresh salmon, can we barbecue?"

"On Friday? I usually go out with Cliff."

"Well, how about including your doctor and Sylvia for dinner? I'll bring a whole salmon."

"That sounds great. I'm sure Cliff will be pleased. He's very fond of salmon."

"I'll call when I get home. Meanwhile, sweet dreams!"

Hanging up, Tracy hoped Cliff wouldn't be difficult about barbecuing here at home. Andy would handle the fire and the fish. Cliff could entertain Sylvia. With that settled in her mind, Tracy fell asleep. Her dreams were confusing. One minute she was assisting Cliff with a minor operation. The next, she was terrified by a newspaper picture of a crashed helicopter. She awoke in a cold sweat.

Chapter V

Cliff wasn't too happy about Tracy's plan to stay home and barbecue salmon instead of going into Mendocino.

"We always go out on Friday," he told Tracy. "Why didn't you plan the barbecue for Saturday?"

"Andy wanted to come Friday. He's bringing fresh salmon. Just once, can't we stay home?"

"You say Sylvia is coming? And Andy will do the barbecuing?"

"Yes," Tracy said.

"In that case, I'll give in this one time."

Having gone to such lengths to win Cliff over, Tracy was upset when Sylvia called to say Andy had been delayed and they couldn't come on Friday, after all.

"But everything is all set up!" Tracy protested.

"I'm sorry." Sylvia didn't really sound sorry. "You realize, I'm sure, that managing one's own business isn't like working for someone else. Andy isn't on a nine-to-five schedule."

"Neither are doctors or nurses, as far as that goes."

"Then you do understand," Sylvia said.

In a resigned tone of voice, Tracy asked, "Did Andy say anything about Saturday? Can we change the day?"

Sylvia hesitated. "I'm not sure. Andy will be tired. Then, too, he's going to be with the mechanic a good part of the day."

"What about the evening? If he's bringing a salmon, he'll want to barbecue it while it's fresh."

"Well, maybe we can make it on Saturday."

"Is Andy there, so I can talk to him?"

"No—no, he isn't." After a long pause, Sylvia said, "I guess you can go ahead and plan for Saturday. Will six o'clock be all right?"

"Six will be ideal."

As Tracy expected, Cliff reacted strongly.

"I told you that helicopter pilot was unreliable! I should have known better than to change my plans. Now what will we do on Friday?"

"Mendocino is still there. We can find someplace to have dinner."

"That isn't the point. I had made reservations at the Little River Inn. You know they're usually booked solid for the weekend."

"Really, Cliff, it isn't any great tragedy if we have to eat someplace other than the Little River Inn. Instead of driving to Mendocino, why don't we go for a horseback ride, then have dinner at the hotel here?"

"Then barbecue on Saturday? Spend all weekend right here in Centerville?"

At the consternation in Cliff's voice, Tracy broke into laughter.

Stiffly Cliff said, "I see nothing funny in wanting a change of scenery."

"I guess you're right. Except I find all the change I need right there. After five days at the clinic, I like peace and quiet. I don't need social stimulation."

"Once we get back to the Bay Area, you'll change your mind. You'll find life so much more exciting."

How could she convince Cliff that she found life more exciting here, with her garden and her horse, than it had ever been? Tracy had spent a year in Japan and two years in Hawaii and she hadn't been anywhere near as happy as she was right here in Centerville. If only Cliff could be happy here, too!

Tracy got up early Saturday morning in order to get in a horseback ride. Molly hadn't been out for several days and danced in impatience while being saddled.

"Molly girl," Tracy said, "stand still! I know you're high-spirited and eager to be off. You can have a good run. Then we'll ride to the top of the ridge. I have to be back in time to clean house and get ready for this evening."

With wind-tossed hair, cheeks rosy, and eyes sparkling, Tracy reined Molly in to gaze, as she did whenever she rode to this outlook, in awe at the panorama spread out before her. She could see Spencer Valley, snug between two mountain ranges, with its vineyards, sparse houses, lumberyard, and grazing sheep. How could anyone prefer the clutter and clatter of an urban area to this? How could she change Cliff's mind and help him see it through her eyes?

Tracy put on designer jeans and a jade-green sweater that evening. As a finishing touch, she added a gold chain and simple gold earrings. Andy's nod of approval brought a flush to her face.

"Green Eyes." Andy nodded again. "Your eyes match your sweater. Or the ocean with the sun filtering through a wave."

Spitefully Sylvia added, "Or the eyes of a green-eyed cat."

"Why, thank you!" Tracy said with a smile. "My favorite cat had green eyes. I could see them in the dark. She was a beautiful white cat and I loved her dearly."

"Tracy has a thing for animals," Cliff confided. "You couldn't pay her a higher compliment."

Sylvia's eyes narrowed and her lips tight-

ened. Then, flashing a bright smile, she took
Cliff's arm.

"I know Tracy will be busy in the kitchen
and Andy will be starting the fire. Why don't
you show me around? Andy has been extra-
vagant in praise of what Tracy has done
here."

As Sylvia and Cliff went down the steps,
Andy turned to Tracy, his brown eyes dancing with mischief.

"Nicely done, Green Eyes! Talking about
cats, Sylvia can be rather feline herself."

"How long have you known her?" Tracy
asked.

"Five years, I'd say. Jim and I were bud-
dies. We often flew together. I will say this.
Sylvia was loyal and really loved Jim. The
only times they weren't together was when
we were sent out of the country."

"Is she happy in Kingsley?"

Andy shrugged. "I'm not sure. I know she's
a help to me. I hate all the bookkeeping and
stuff like that. Sylvia is a good businesswoman. She has an inborn aptitude for running things." He smiled wryly. "She'd like to
run me. No way! I'm a free spirit and I expect
to remain free."

At these words Tracy's heart did a flip-flop
and some of the radiance went out of the day.
But why should it matter to her that Andy
wanted to remain free? She had no designs

on him, even though she found him irresistibly attractive. She still wanted to share her future with Cliff...at the clinic.

Andy went to his car and returned with an ice chest in which he had the salmon and two bottles of wine.

"Are you going to barbecue the salmon whole, or cut it into steaks?" Tracy asked.

"I'll do it whole. It doesn't take long. I have a special marinade I use." He held up a bottle of wine with the flush of a ripe peach. "Pearl wine. It has a delicate taste, just right with salmon."

Tracy's spirits soared as she worked along with Andy preparing the dinner. This was the kind of entertaining she enjoyed. She remained in the kitchen, fixing a fruit salad and some other things, while Andy moved back and forth between the kitchen and the deck. Sylvia and Cliff didn't return until dinner was ready.

"I'm really impressed," Sylvia told Tracy. "Still, I can't imagine myself living here alone. You must get bored and feel lonely."

"Strangely, I don't. My work takes a lot out of me. When I get home at night, I'm quite content if there's time to go for a ride on Molly or putter in my garden. Then, too, there's so much I still need to do to improve the house. Anyway, people in Centerville are very friendly. I could go out nearly every evening if I wanted to. Staying home is my choice."

"She'll change when we move back to the Bay Area," Cliff said.

Startled, Andy turned to Tracy. "Are you leaving Centerville? Somehow I got the impression you had put down roots and expected to live here indefinitely."

"Cliff wants a more challenging and lucrative practice. I, myself, am content and happy right here."

"I see," Andy said slowly.

They all enjoyed the dinner. Cliff declared the barbecued salmon the best he had ever tasted.

"I caught it myself," Andy told him.

"Do you go fishing often?" Cliff asked.

"No. But I managed to get out for a little while. Ran into a fellow with his own boat. What I do enjoy is diving for abalone."

"He's a regular nut about it," Sylvia volunteered. "Gets up in the middle of the night to drive to the coast, then stays in the water longer than anyone else!"

"Not really," Andy contradicted. "I never go abaloning alone. It isn't safe." He turned to Cliff. "Would you like to go with me sometime?"

"I think not," Cliff replied. "We won't be around much longer, and I don't want to invest in a wet suit."

"I'd like to go with you," Tracy said. "I think diving would be exciting."

Grinning, Andy said, "Oh, it is! I started diving in high school. In fact, I had planned on becoming a navy frogman, but I got side-tracked. I ended up in the air instead of at the bottom of the ocean."

"Then you'll take me with you sometime?" Tracy asked.

Cliff said, "Indeed he won't! I gave in to your folly of buying a horse, but diving for abalone is going too far."

Tracy's face flamed. "I'll go if I want to! Dad promised to teach me while we were in Hawaii, but he never got around to it. Now that I have a chance, I intend to follow through."

"We'll discuss this later," Cliff said, his eyes cold and angry.

Tracy, gathering up the dishes to take them to the kitchen, felt Andy's probing gaze. What had made Cliff assert himself so forcefully? He had never before, at least in public, been this possessive.

Anyway, if Andy ever asked her, she would go abaloning with him. She had made up her mind to that.

They lingered over dessert and coffee until, yawning, Andy stood up.

"I hate to break this up, but I've had a rugged week. I'm for home and bed!"

"We really should help Tracy clean up," Sylvia protested.

"That isn't necessary," Tracy assured her. "I rather like to clean up when everyone's gone. I take my time and putter. Also, I know what it is to drive over the hill this time of night. I've done it often enough!"

Andy took Tracy's hand in both of his. "Thanks for humoring me. Everything was great."

"Thank you for the salmon! It was a real treat."

"I must agree with Tracy," Cliff said. "The salmon was a real treat. I'm sorry I haven't gone out fishing. Maybe I'll get back later and have a try at it."

"When do you leave?" Sylvia asked.

"My contract expires the end of August."

"Then you've found a place to resettle?" Andy inquired.

"It isn't firmed up yet. I hope to settle in San Mateo."

"And take Tracy with you?"

Cliff shrugged. "Tracy's buried herself here in Centerville long enough."

Cliff stood with Tracy and watched Sylvia and Andy drive away.

"Sylvia's a smart woman," Cliff remarked. "I think she runs that helicopter outfit and him, too. Carlton's lucky to have her."

Lips pinched in silence, Tracy made no

reply. Even Andy admitted that Sylvia was a smart businesswoman and a big help in running the business. But that didn't mean she ran Andy's private life!

They stood for a few minutes in silence.

Then Cliff said, "I'll be running along, too." His good-night kiss had more fervor than usual. "I miss you, Tracy, when we're not together."

After checking to make sure the gate was locked, Tracy went back into the house. Sighing deeply, she filled the sink with water and started washing the dishes. She would miss Cliff. It would be hard to adjust to working with another doctor. But did she love him enough to give up everything she had here?

She had the kitchen clean and had started up to bed when the phone rang. A call at this hour of the night always set her heart to thumping even though she was used to meeting emergency situations. It was Andy.

"I knew you wouldn't be in bed yet," he said. "Anyway, I called to ask what gives with you and the doctor? Are you leaving with him when he goes?"

"I—don't know."

"What do you mean, you don't know?"

"Just that. I've more or less taken it for granted that Cliff and I would continue as a team. We're used to working together. I don't know what it would be like without him."

"But you like it here, don't you?"

"Indeed I do! I'm very happy with both my work and my rancho."

"Then why are you planning on leaving?"

"I'm not planning on leaving."

"Now you sound just like a woman! Anyway, I'm glad you plan on sticking around, and I hope you won't let the doctor talk you into changing your mind. Another reason I called was to ask if you meant it when you said you'd like to go abalone diving with me?"

"Of course, I meant it. Would I have to buy a wet suit?"

"Maybe we can borrow one. Try it first before investing too much money. We need to wait for the full moon when the tide is right. I'll try to let you know in advance, but we may have to go on short notice. Work comes first, recreation second. Sometimes I think maybe I'm doing too well!"

"You don't mean that."

"Of course not. I'd be singing the blues loud and long if I couldn't keep both of my machines in the air. But I'm about due for an overhaul on the Bell. That will keep it on the ground for two or three days."

"Will the moon be full?"

"I'm going to try to schedule my time to fit the moon. I can't always arrange things the way I want. Our work isn't all scheduled in advance, you realize."

"I know! I've had to cancel more than one engagement because of my work." After a pause, she added, "I really enjoyed this evening. Having friends in to dinner is my favorite form of entertainment."

"Mine, too. And, Tracy, I'm glad we see eye to eye on that!"

Chapter VI

Cliff surprised Tracy by announcing that he would be gone over the Fourth of July. In fact, he'd leave Centerville on the second.

"I have a hot lead about an opening in a medical clinic in San Mateo," he said. "But you know that. Well, there are still some people I have to see and so forth. I'd take over the family-practice unit. Benjie Michaels, an internist, is the son of the clinic director. We were in medical school together. I ran into Benjie in San Francisco. He told me about their plans to expand. I sent in my application and have an appointment with Dr. Calvin Michaels on July fifth."

"But you plan on leaving on the second?"

"Yes. You don't mind, do you? Someone has to be here on Tuesday and Wednesday and you enjoy the local entertainment more than the city."

Tracy suppressed a feeling of annoyance. How many times had she filled in for Cliff while he took off? It was partly her fault, of course. Cliff had asked her to go with him

58

several times, but she had refused. Now what
could she say?

The clinic would be closed on Thursday, the
Fourth of July. With Cliff gone, Tracy made
no plans for special holiday activities. Instead she would go for a long ride on Molly
and work in her yard. Feeling restless and,
unusual for her, lonely, she found the pros-
pect not as alluring as it would once have
been. She welcomed Andy's call.

"What are you doing on the Fourth of
July?" he asked. "I have to stick around. Sylvia asked for a few days off from work. Someone has to be here. There's a barbecue and
fireworks at the fairground. Would you mind
going to that?"

"I'd love it," Tracy assured him. "They put
on a good fireworks display. I hear the food is
good, too, although I've never gone to the
barbecue."

"Why don't you come early, and I'll show
you my operation. You don't mind meeting
me here at the airport, do you?"

"Of course not. Also, I'll enjoy hearing
more about your work."

"Good! I'll look for you around two o'clock."

The weather had been getting hot. Tracy
noticed that the creek running through her
property had dried up, leaving a bed of gravel
and sand, while the grass had burned brown.
She had to carry water to Molly and gave her

alfalfa to supplement the sparse, dry grass in the corral. There had been reports of fires in various areas. As the hot spell continued, Tracy became uneasy.

On the Fourth of July she got up early to go horseback riding, then spent two hours in her garden. After lunch she showered, then dressed in white slacks with a white top. Bidding Molly good-by, she got in her car, a four-year-old Toyota, and drove to Kingsley.

As she approached the airport on the outskirts of the town, she noted the lack of air traffic although there were a number of small planes on the ground. She found Andy, feet propped on his desk, talking on the phone. He waved her to a seat facing him.

"That was Tim," he said, replacing the receiver and sitting up straight in his chair. "He flew a V.I.P., the local senator, to a big salmon barbecue. Tim's going to stick around to fly the senator back to San Francisco. That means I have to be available. I hope you don't mind spending the afternoon here at the airport."

"I don't mind. I'd like to learn all about your business. It sounds fascinating."

"I find it so. However, there's a lot of routine even with helicopters. And the paperwork! It will really pile up while Sylvia is in San Francisco."

"Oh? That's where Cliff is. He has an appointment in San Mateo on the fifth, but he went early."

"So you got stuck and had to work?" Andy asked.

"I don't mind, really. I can handle most things that come up. That's why Cliff wants to leave. He feels our clinic isn't exciting enough."

"But you do need a doctor," Andy said.

"Of course. As a nurse practitioner, I'm limited to certain things. There are many procedures only a doctor can do, and we have enough people in Spencer Valley to keep the two of us busy."

"When will the doctor be back?"

"Sunday at the latest. Why?" Tracy asked.

Andy pointed to a calendar hanging on the wall. "Full moon Tuesday. I'm arranging my schedule to go abaloning. Can you get away to go with me?"

"We won't be all day, or will we?"

"How early can you get up? I like to be in the water by sunrise. We should be back by ten A.M. or thereabouts."

"Great! I'll plan on going to work at noon. Cliff can cover for me in the morning."

Andy stood up. "Now to show you my pride and joy!"

He led the way outside and walked to a helicopter standing not far from the entrance to the building. Tracy smiled as he ran a hand along the nose of the insect-like machine, patting it as she would pat Molly.

"This is a light utility helicopter, a Bell, very practical, and the best machine for our operation. We use the Bell as an air ambulance, for aerial photography, lift jobs, and passenger service. It accommodates up to four people. Tim has Little Brother, a two-seated copter, which we use for single passengers, forest surveys, and such."

Moving on, Andy pointed out various features of the helicopter.

"What has been your most interesting assignment since you got involved in this work?" Tracy asked.

"Flying in a movie. When I first got out of the army, I worked for a company that supplied helicopters to movie makers. Jim and I had made plans to own our own company, so I didn't stay with that outfit long."

A beep-beep sounded and Andy removed his beeper from a pocket. Then he ran to the phone, Tracy at his heels.

There was a highway emergency. When Andy got all the details, he turned to Tracy.

"Am I glad you're here! You can take Vance's place as my paramedic!" He dashed toward the helicopter.

Running to keep up, Tracy said, "Andy! What is it? Where are we going?"

"Big car pileup on Highway 101—toward

Eureka. Fire in the hills. Smoke so thick it blacked out the highway!"

"But—but I've never been in a helicopter!"

"You've gone on ambulance runs! No different. Splints, medicine kit, everything on board. I'll brief you while we're in the air."

Breathless, her pulse racing, Tracy took her seat beside Andy. He handed her a helmet and showed her how to buckle herself in her seat. She watched in wide-eyed fascination as the engines roared to life, startled by the noise, shaken by the vibrations.

Watching her, Andy grinned. "Noisy, isn't it?"

"You can say that again!"

"Noise is, unfortunately, one of the drawbacks to helicopter use. When they lick that, you'll see more helicopters in the air."

It seemed strange to Tracy to rise straight up without a run down the runway and a gradual climb upward. Visibility from the bubble-like cabin was excellent as Andy headed north.

After a few minutes, Tracy asked him what to expect when they reached their destination.

"It'll be routine first aid and rescue," he informed her. "Actually, we'll load the patients assigned to us and head back. Others at the scene will have things well in control when we arrive." His voice grew somber. "Look,

smoke! And flames! I wonder how large an
area the fire has ravaged."

Tracy, too, saw the billowing smoke and
the orange flames. She couldn't control a
shudder of fear. What if the fire spread to
Centerville? She wouldn't be there to get
Molly to safety. And her home. What if it
burned down? No! That couldn't happen! She
saw a circling airplane and watched as it
dipped low over the trees, releasing a spray
of chemicals.

"That's a Forestry plane," Andy said.
"There must be a number of ground units
working with the air coverage. They'll have
the fire contained soon, I'm sure."

"I hope so!"

"Tracy! Look!"

She looked where Andy was pointing.
"How awful! How could such a thing happen?"

As the helicopter started its descent, Tracy
continued staring at the tangle of cars ob-
structing the highway below. She had never
seen such carnage. As they dipped lower, she
could see police cars, fire trucks, and ambulances, with people running in all directions.
Tears filmed her eyes. What a sad Fourth of
July this had turned out to be for so many
vacationers!

A highway patrolman told Andy where to
land and had the door open almost before the

helicopter touched ground.

He said, "We have two cases that need immediate medical care. One with possible in-
ternal bleeding, and another with a head
injury. The hospital in Kingsley is expecting
them."

With a speed that left Tracy breathless, the
patients were placed on stretchers and lifted
into the helicopter. She took her place beside
them, ready to check vital signs and admin-
ister such care as they might need en route to
the hospital. Her primary concern was pre-
venting the first patient from going into
shock.

Within minutes the helicopter settled gently on the helipad at the Kingsley Community Hospital. Attendants awaited them with
wheeled stretchers. The two patients were
placed on these and rushed inside. After a
few terse words with the doctor, Tracy got
back in the helicopter, the engines growled,
and once again they were airborne.

"What kind of cases will we have this
time?" Tracy asked.

Andy shrugged. "Fractures, probably.
There were over twenty cars in the pileup.
They're still pulling people out."

From the care with which the next patients
were handled, Tracy realized one must have
suffered a neck injury with possible damage
to the spinal cord, while the second one had a

leg and arm splinted. These patients would
also be taken to Kingsley Community Hospital. Two ambulances left the scene of the accident as the helicopter lifted into the air.

"This will be our last run," Andy said.
"Those ambulances are heading for Santa
Rosa. I guess Kingsley has all they can
handle."

Soon Tracy was helping to get the patients
inside the hospital while Andy stayed with
the helicopter. After asking about the first
two patients and learning both were still in
surgery, Tracy climbed in beside Andy to return to the airfield.

"Some Fourth of July!" Andy commented.
He reached over and squeezed Tracy's hand.
"You were great. I'm mighty glad you were
along. Even though I can think of more interesting ways to spend our time together."

"I'm glad we were available to help." Suddenly Tracy shivered. "Those poor people!
Andy, I've never seen anything so awful. And
all caused by smoke from a forest fire. I
wonder how far the fire will spread."

"We saw the fire bombers out, and fire
units from miles around were rushed to help
fight the blaze. It will be contained very soon,
I'm sure."

Tracy was still shivering when Andy
helped her down from the helicopter. Smiling
tenderly, he gathered her close in his arms.

"Poor darling. I guess this was hard on you." He bent down and kissed her. "I'll make it up to you. We'll have dinner, then watch the fireworks."

Tracy went back into the office, still shivering, while Andy secured the helicopter for the night.

After a while he came in whistling. Hadn't the accident moved him at all? Meeting Tracy's accusing gaze, Andy came over and again put his arms around her.

"I wouldn't have let you go with me if I had realized it would upset you." He brushed her lips in a feathery kiss. "We'll have dinner and put all of that behind us."

"I'm—I'm sorry. It's just—well, the ambulance runs I've been on were either medical cases or a simple one-car accident. Somehow seeing it from the air—looking down on all that wreckage..." A shudder racked her body. "It was a replay of my nightmares when Dad crashed."

Andy kissed her more soundly. "Green Eyes, your father was doing exactly what he wanted to do, or he wouldn't have been a test pilot. He knew the risks. So do people who drive our crowded highways."

Face flushed, eyes sparking, Tracy pulled away. "None of the people in those cars expected a forest fire! That was something beyond their control."

"True. But I'll give you odds that most of them were driving beyond the speed limit." Once again Andy gathered Tracy close, his cheek resting against her hair. "You'll probably never see anything like that again, so put it out of your mind. Just remember it's a holiday and that we're celebrating and are together. As far as I'm concerned, being with you is what really counts."

Chapter VII

Tracy and Andy reached the fairground barely in time to be served.

"Ten minutes later and you wouldn't have gotten anything to eat," the man who served them spareribs said. "Anyway, enjoy your dinner. The fireworks start as soon as it's dark."

Much to Tracy's surprise, she was ravenous. The typical Fourth of July fare—spareribs, corn on the cob, and watermelon—was excellent.

"That was good," Andy said as they tossed their paper plates into the trash can. "Now for the fireworks!"

They took their seats on the grandstand. Dusk hadn't yet deepened into dark. Both Tracy and Andy settled back to wait.

"This reminds me of my teens," Andy said. "Only, we watched from the beach. We always had a fire and roasted wieners."

"My first real Fourth was the year I came here. My folks were out of the country so much. Dad always said we'd have an old-

69

fashioned Fourth, but it never worked out."

"You really miss your father, don't you?"

"Dad and I were very close. When he died, my world seemed to stop."

"What about your mother? Didn't you get along with her?"

"Mom's swell. Only—well, she and I don't have the same closeness I had with Dad. She and my sister were closer. In fact, Annamarie still lives at home. She studied drama at college and wants to be an actress. So far she's had a few minor parts on TV."

Conversation stopped as the first rocket finally exploded in a burst of vivid color. A long, drawn-out "Ahhhhh" died away as the last spark faded and darkness again claimed the world. Almost before people caught their breath, another rocket exploded in a sunburst.

Tracy laughed in delight. "I love this! I'm enjoying it as much as I did my first Fourth of July here in Kingsley."

"I hope the present company accounts for at least part of your enjoyment."

"Of course! Oh! Look!"

The fireworks grew more and more spectacular. And the display was over all too soon.

"Now I feel that I've had another real Fourth of July!"

Andy slipped his arm around her and

hugged her. "I'm glad you enjoyed the evening. It makes up for the afternoon. I'm still glad that you were here to go with me. Maybe we can team up."

"Oh, no! I'm perfectly content with my work at the clinic. That's what I trained for and I find it very satisfying. And I'm helping people who really need me."

"That's important to you, isn't it?" Andy said.

"Yes. Isn't it to you?"

Andy shrugged. "If they need my helicopter services and can pay what I ask. I don't run a charity outfit."

Tracy turned down Andy's suggestion that they stop for coffee.

"I have to get home," she told him. "Tomorrow will be a full day. Especially with Cliff away."

"I'm sorry you have to drive all that way alone. I didn't think about it being so late when I invited you for the day."

"I don't mind driving alone. I've driven from Centerville to Kingsley so often, I know every turn in the road. There's no need for you to wory."

"Well, call me when you get home. And don't forget—I'm looking forward to you diving for abalone with me!"

"I won't forget. I'll clear it with Cliff on Monday, then call you."

The drive home through the velvety night seemed short to Tracy.

She smiled in anticipation, thinking about Tuesday. She hoped Cliff wouldn't offer any objections.

As it turned out, he phoned her Sunday evening. Tracy could feel and hear the excitement in his voice.

"Things went better than I dared hope! The elder Dr. Michaels and I hit it off first rate. He's a lot like Benjie. It isn't firmed up yet, but I have every reason to be hopeful."

"That's great, Cliff. If it's what you really want."

"Of course, that's what I want!"

"Won't it still be family practice? You won't be doing heart transplants or anything like that. Won't it be pretty much the same as practicing here?"

"Hardly!" he said.

"It seems to me families have the same problems no matter where they live. People get old and have related illnesses, women have babies who get sick, teen-agers have their share of ills."

"I realize all of that. Even so practicing in an urban area is far different from practicing in a rural area. And look at the cultural advantages! Anyway, let's drop that. I have something to tell you that will make you see things in a totally different light."

"Oh? What's that?"

"I'll discuss it with you in the morning. I'm beat and want to get to bed."

Then something prompted Tracy to say, "By the way, Sylvia Duncan spent the Fourth of July in San Francisco. You didn't by any chance run into her, did you?"

There was a cold silence. Then Cliff said stiffly, "It just so happened that we did run into each other. In fact, we stayed at the same hotel."

"A mere coincidence," Tracy observed.

"I would call it that. Sylvia asked me where I stayed when I went to the city. She had some business to attend to. We did go to dinner and a play. Incidentally, what did you do on the Fourth?"

"I went to Kingsley. Andy invited me to go to the barbecue and watch the fireworks. It turned out to be more exciting than I anticipated. Did you read about the twenty-car pileup on Highway 101? I went with Andy to transport some of the injured motorists to Kingsley Community."

"You took charge of the patients? That seems exactly the kind of stunt he would pull. And I don't suppose he paid you."

"Pay me? Don't be silly! I was glad I was there to go with him."

"You won't be around for him to pull such a stunt again, so I guess there's no need to say anything. Don't forget! I have something exciting to tell you in the morning."

Tracy replaced the receiver, a puzzled frown wrinkling her forehead. Sometimes she found Cliff hard to understand. Had it been coincidence that he and Sylvia had stayed at the same hotel in San Francisco? Or had they gone to the city together? And what did Cliff have to tell her in the morning?

The following day Tracy was surprised to find Cliff waiting for her when she arrived at the clinic.

"This is unexpected," she greeted him. "How come you're here so early?"

"I told you I wanted to talk to you," he replied, leading the way to his office. He sat down at his desk and motioned Tracy to a chair.

"Now," Tracy prompted, "what's this all about?"

A wide smile spread over Cliff's face. "You're going with me to San Mateo if I go!"

Tracy blinked in surprise. "I am?"

"Yes. Dr. Michaels told me they're going to add a nurse practitioner to their family-practice service, and I told him all about you! He wants to see you and I promised we'd meet with him next week."

"You made this promise without talking to me first?"

"Oh, come now! This is what we both want! Why, we could work together there just as we're doing here."

"But, Cliff, I don't want to leave Centerville! I've told you that a dozen times."

"But you've also led me to believe you loved me. Naturally I've assumed you would do whatever I wanted."

Tracy stared at him blankly. Had she really thought she was in love with Cliff? Had she? She still couldn't imagine working without him beside her. But did she want that badly enough to give up all she had here and move to San Mateo?

Maria poked her head through the door.

"Dr. Cliff, Mrs. Anderson is here. She called every day you were gone."

The doctor stood up and so did Tracy. He paused and brushed her lips with his.

"You don't have to give me an answer today, Tracy. Think it over and we'll talk again tomorrow."

Tracy walked to her office in a daze. Most nurses, she knew, would jump at the chance to work in a prestigious clinic in the Bay Area. Was there something wrong with her that she liked the rural setting and felt happier here than she had ever felt before? If Cliff left and another doctor came, would working here be the same? What answer would she give Cliff tomorrow?

It wasn't until late afternoon that Tracy remembered she hadn't made arrangements not to come in until noon the next day. She looked at her appointment book, glad that there was nothing Cliff couldn't take care of for her. She would be sure to be back by noon. She went to Cliff's office to talk to him about the abalone diving.

"You aren't really serious, are you?" he asked. "Of course, you aren't going diving for abalone! I thought I made that clear when we discussed it before."

Anger raced through Tracy, crimsoning her face and bringing a sparkle to her green eyes.

"I'm going if I want to! You have nothing to say about what I do."

"It's too dangerous. I won't let you risk your life."

"But I'll be with Andy!"

"That's part of the problem. He's reckless and takes unnecessary chances. Sylvia told me about some of his exploits. You are not going with him, and that's final."

Seething with anger, Tracy returned to her office. A patient was waiting, so she had to put off phoning. When she did call, Sylvia answered the phone.

"I'm sorry, but Andy isn't here...No, I don't know when he will be back. Of course, I'll tell him you called."

When Andy hadn't returned her call by the

time she was ready to go home, she called again. There was no answer. Certainly Sylvia would have told her if Andy had been on a helicopter run. Hadn't he told her the overhaul on the Bell would ground them for a few days? He always carried a beeper if he was at the airfield. Could he have changed his mind about tomorrow?

Tracy had so looked forward to diving for abalone. What could have changed his mind? Maybe he hadn't been able to borrow the wet suit for her and decided to go without her. But he should have called.

By ten o'clock that night Tracy still hadn't reached Andy and he had not called her. She decided to try one more time, then give up. He answered on the first ring.

"Oh, Tracy." He sounded surprised.

"Andy, I've been trying to reach you since this afternoon. Didn't Sylvia give you my message?"

"No. But then I was out of the office. I'm sorry you changed your mind about going for abalone with me. I'd looked forward to our being together."

"But I haven't changed my mind! That's why I'm calling. To ask what time you'll be here."

"Dr. Sampson gave me to understand, in no uncertain terms, that you would not be going with me. I didn't realize you two were planning on being married, or that you would leave Centerville when he left."

"Cliff phoned—and told you that?"

"Emphatically!"

"But—but—" Tracy stammered futilely. What could she say? She had given Cliff reason to think she wanted to be married. Could she deny it to Andy?

"Then it's true," Andy said. "I'm sorry about tomorrow. However, Sylvia has decided to go with me. She's never wanted to before. Another couple, friends of ours, will join us. The way things are going, I'll be grounded until Thursday, so we'll have an abalone feed at Sylvia's on Wednesday. How about you and your doctor joining us?"

"Since he's running my life, you'd better check with him!"

Slamming the receiver down, Tracy jumped up and began pacing the room. What right did Cliff have to call Andy? She had really wanted to dive for abalone. Or did she just want to be with Andy? Of course, that was the only reason Sylvia had decided to take her place. So she could be with Andy.

But why had Sylvia followed Cliff to San Francisco? Did she really have business there and was their being together only a coincidence, after all? And what did she, Tracy, really feel for Cliff? She had been so sure he would want to stay in Centerville just as she did. She couldn't give up Molly and the rancho. No, not even to marry Cliff and go with him to San Mateo.

Chapter VIII

Tracy spent a restless night and at the first hint of sunrise she was at the window, looking out. Would Sylvia really don a wet suit and go in the water with Andy? The more Tracy thought about Cliff calling Andy and telling him she would not accompany him this morning, the more angry she became. Who did Dr. Clifford L. Sampson think he was?

When had she given him permission to take charge of her life? She would make it clear to him today that she would not be leaving Centerville. Which meant there would be no wedding.

This thought brought more relief than sorrow. That meant Tracy hadn't been as much in love as she had thought she was! She had become so used to working with Cliff that she hadn't wanted to even think about working with anyone else.

Did Andy have any bearing on her decision? Too bad if he did. Cliff had cooled that, if there had been anything there. Her anger rekindled. She would tell Dr. Sampson just what she thought of his high-handed action!

However, if she had expected Cliff to be sorry, she was disappointed.

He said, "What is there to be upset about? I can't imagine anyone getting up in the middle of the night, dressing in one of those tight rubber suits, and getting into that cold water just to pry a shellfish off a rock. Anyone has to be a nut to want to do that."

"Then I guess you can class Sylvia as a nut. She went in my place."

"Sylvia?" Cliff sounded incredulous. "I don't believe it! She wouldn't do anything that foolish."

Tracy stalked to her own office. Arguing with Cliff wouldn't get her any place. Maybe she could talk to Andy and arrange to go with him next time he dove for abalone. But who knew when that might be?

She was surprised when Cliff appeared at her office door later that afternoon.

"You were right. Sylvia did go abaloning with Andy. Only—" A complacent smile spread across his face. "Your helicopter pilot overlooked one little detail."

"And what was that?" Tracy asked.

"Abalone can only be taken during April, May, June, August, September, October, and November. Not July! Instead of diving for abalone, they went out on a fishing boat. Sylvia

refused to join them. She said it was cold and
foggy, and she had to sit in the car until a
cafe opened. No more abalone trips for her!
And no abalone feed tomorrow. Sylvia said
that instead they'll barbecue red snapper.
We're invited to join them for dinner at her
place."

Tracy's heart skipped a beat. Then Andy
wasn't upset! He still wanted her to come to
dinner tomorrow. Or had that been Sylvia's
idea, not Andy's?

"I think that would be fun. What time do
they want us?"

"Dinner is at seven. We'll leave here about
six."

On Wednesday Tracy left the office early.
She rushed home to see to Molly before getting ready for the evening. Then she showered and changed into a cool-looking green
outfit. It wasn't long before Cliff arrived.

"I wish we were going to Mendocino instead of Kingsley," he said. He sounded like a
spoiled child.

Sylvia lived in a white bungalow with
green shutters on a tree-shaded street a short
distance from downtown Kingsley. A neatly
trimmed hedge enclosed a small front yard
with a velvety green lawn and colorful
flowers.

Andy answered their ring and led them
through the living room to the spacious back-

yard. His casual greeting and impersonal manner hit Tracy like a blast of cold air. Then inviting them today had been Sylvia's idea. Andy would rather she hadn't come.

Sylvia hurried out of the kitchen to greet them. "I'm so glad you could join us," she said, her eyes on Cliff. Again Tracy felt it would have been better if she hadn't come. But what was Sylvia's game? Was she trying to make Andy jealous by pretending an interest in Cliff?

They were introduced to the other guests, Fred Howell, a young lawyer, and his wife, Evelyn, and Tim and his wife, Peggy.

"I've been hoping to see you," Tim said, holding Tracy's hand as he grinned down at her. "He owes me, the boss does! I told him about the beautiful nurse at the Centerville clinic, so he pulled rank on me and decided to fly the heart patient to the vets' hospital himself." He shook his head dolefully. "I'm used to listening to him rave about the girls he meets. But now all I hear is Tracy Nichols!"

Laughing, Tracy said, "Aren't you exaggerating a little?"

Solemnly raising his hand, Tim said, "It's true! Now I have more to listen to. Not only are you beautiful, you know your stuff, medically! That pileup on the Fourth was something, wasn't it?"

"I certainly got a new perspective, seeing it from the air," Tracy said.

"What scared me," Peggy said, "was the fire. What if it had spread to Kingsley?"

"I thought of that," Tracy said. "We're fortunate they were able to contain the fire when they did."

"Let's hope there won't be any more fires this summer," Evelyn said.

Sylvia appeared with a tray and offered Tracy a glass of wine.

"I hope you like this," she said. "This is rather special. A gift from one of our customers." As Tracy took a stemmed glass, she added, "Dinner will be ready soon. Too bad it won't be abalone. Andy and Fred are both mortified. They knew abalone can't be taken during July, but in their eagerness, they forgot—until they realized why we were the only divers there. Anyway, that's my one and only attempt at abalone diving. Never again!"

"I'd still like to go with Andy next time he goes," Tracy said.

Sylvia shrugged. "The pleasure's all yours."

"Is there anything I can do to help?" Tracy asked.

"No, I don't think so. Andy and Fred have an agreement. Fred cleans the fish and Andy cooks it. Everything else is ready to put on

the table. It's such a lovely evening, I felt we
had to eat outdoors."

Tracy agreed. The evening, cooling from
the heat of the afternoon, was ideal for being
outside with friends.

They were seated when Andy came out
carrying a large platter of fish.

"Baked, stuffed red snapper instead of abalone," he said. "Sorry to disappoint you."

"That red snapper looks delicious," Tracy
said. "I just wish I had gone with you."

"You didn't miss anything," Sylvia told her.
"It was cold and miserable. Nothing would
have gotten me on that boat!"

"I would have gone," Tracy said. "I like
deep-sea fishing. I used to go with Dad."

"There will be another time," Andy con-
soled her. "In August we can dive for abalone. Maybe then you can arrange to go with
us."

He looked questioningly at Cliff. The doctor merely shrugged. Tracy's lips were set in
a firm line.

"Just let me know and I'll join you. That's
something I've wanted to do for a long time,
just as I wanted to go snorkling in Hawaii."

"One can hardly equate snorkling in the
warm waters off Hawaii with diving for abalone along the northern coast of California,"
Sylvia replied.

"That's true," Andy agreed. "There you

would probably dive for the pleasure of seeing what's on the ocean floor. I dive for abalone because I like them as food. Love them,
in fact."

As dinner progressed, Andy kept them entertained with stories of his exploits as a
scuba diver in Southern California before he
entered the armed forces.

"It's a whole new world down there," he
said. "One time we found a sunken ship. No
treasure, though. Then another time I came
face to face with a shark. Fortunately he was
as startled as I was. You never saw anyone
surface as fast as I did!"

During the evening, Tracy's look strayed to
Andy frequently. Not once did her gaze meet
his gaze. As far as she could tell, if he'd had
any interest in her, it had vanished.

Sylvia and Evelyn insisted that, since
Andy and Fred had cooked dinner, they
would clear up and do the dishes. The others
moved to comfortable chairs. All except Cliff.

"I don't know when I've had a more enjoyable evening," he said. "However, it's time we
headed back over the hill."

Andy glanced at his watch. "It's early yet.
There's no need to rush away. Is there,
Tracy?"

Burningly aware of his mocking gaze,
Tracy stood up and moved to Cliff's side.

"If Cliff is ready to leave, so am I."

"I have rather a full schedule tomorrow

and I'm sure Tracy does, too. We really do have to be on our way."

Andy walked to the car with them. Cliff walked around to the driver's side while Andy opened the door for Tracy.

In a low voice, he said, "Good wishes may be in order, Green Eyes. Only, I don't give up all that easy. You'll be hearing from me."

Without giving Tracy time to reply, he closed the car door, waved, and went back inside. Tracy, aware of the wild fluttering in her chest, but unaware of the joy radiating from her face, wondered at Cliff's frown.

"What in the world do you and Sylvia see in that fellow?" he asked. "He's just a show-off. All that talk about scuba diving! And his exploits as a helicopter pilot. If there had been a war, he would have claimed to have won it single-handed."

Eyes narrowed, Tracy asked quietly, "You aren't jealous, are you?"

Cliff snorted. "Me? Jealous of a helicopter pilot? Don't be ridiculous!" He concentrated on a sharp curve. "I told you Sylvia had more sense than to get in a wet suit and go in the water."

"What does that prove? Neither did the others go diving. But she did get up in the middle of the night to go with Andy. You had no right to call and say I wouldn't go with him."

"We've been over all of that. Besides, what

would be the use of going one time? Once
you're settled in your new job in San Mateo,
you'll forget all such nonsense."

Tracy gazed at Cliff in shocked disbelief.
How could she have worked with him for four
years and not seen how stubborn and self-
centered he was? He still didn't believe that
she meant it when she said she was going to
remain here in Centerville. He was blind to
anything but his own desires.

Realizing Molly was due to have her colt,
Tracy became concerned and made a habit of
coming home during the middle of the day to
see that all was well. The vet had assured her
the birth should be perfectly normal.

Cliff scoffed at her concern. "All this fuss
over a horse! It's ridiculous. And don't forget
that we're driving to San Mateo on Friday.
Dr. Michaels will wait at his office until we
get there."

"But, Cliff, I don't want to go for an interview. I told you that."

"Nonsense! Of course, you'll go. I want you
to at least meet and talk to Dr. Michaels. And
see the setup they have. All new, modern
diagnostic equipment. Everything to work
with. It's a dream situation."

"Not my dream! My dream has been realized right here. There must be a dozen or
more modern, well-equipped clinics in San

Mateo. Here there was none. What we did really counted."

"I'll admit putting it all together was a challenge. Now it's all routine. I'm ready to move on and so should you be." As Tracy started to protest further, he added, "You owe it to me to at least go for the interview. It may have an effect on whether or not I'm accepted."

"Well, when you put it that way. Just don't pin your hopes on my moving with you."

Cliff smiled smugly. "Wait until you see the setup there. Be sure and tell Maria not to schedule you any patients later than eleven-thirty. We need to be on the road by one in order to assure reaching San Mateo before five."

"We'll have to drive back right after seeing Dr. Michaels. I can't be away overnight."

"That's ridiculous! Why do you think I made the appointment for a Friday?"

"You should have cleared it with me. Anyway, I can't be away overnight. Molly is too close to delivery."

"That damned horse! You're going to have to get rid of her. And stop worrying. She'll be all right until we get back on Saturday."

Friday morning Tracy went to check on Molly before going to work. Molly nuzzled her in greeting. Everything looked normal. Molly wasn't ready yet to have her colt.

"I'm going to have to go out of town," Tracy said to the horse. "Don't you dare go into labor while I'm gone!"

After debating whether to take extra clothes and change at the clinic rather than take time to come home, Tracy decided it would be easier just to change at home. She laid everything out on her bed. It wouldn't take long and she would feel much better about how she looked.

The morning went well for Tracy. She saw her last patient out the door right at twelve. Cliff didn't fare as well. He got tied up with a last-mintue emergency.

"Tell Dr. Cliff I'll meet him back here before one," Tracy told Maria. "That will be faster than having him come for me."

She drove into her yard, surprised that Molly wasn't at her usual place by the fence. Nor did the horse come when Tracy walked toward the corral. She quickened her steps, assailed by a sudden feeling of apprehension.

"Molly!" she called.

At an answering whinny from within the shelter, Tracy began to run. She found the mare, apparently in distress, huddled in the corner.

"Molly, what is it?"

Placing her hand on the mare's side, she could feel the muscles in contraction. Molly had gone into labor, but the colt wasn't coming normally. She would have to call the vet. She put her arms around the mare's neck.

"Molly girl, you need help. I'll phone Dr. Graves and get him here as fast as I can."

Fortunately Dr. Graves was in his office. "I'll be there as soon as possible," he assured Tracy.

She hurried back to stay with Molly, all else pushed out of her mind.

Tracy winced each time a contraction tore at the mare. If only there was something she could do! Why wasn't Dr. Graves here by now? Something had to be done for Molly soon!

Soon after the doctor arrived, another car pulled up. A car door slammed. Tracy glanced over to see who it was and put her hand to her mouth in dismay. Cliff! She had completely forgotten. Not wanting a confrontation in front of Dr. Graves, Tracy went to meet him.

"Do you realize what time it is?" Cliff demanded. "We should have been on our way thirty minutes ago."

"I'm sorry, Cliff. When I got home I found Molly in labor. She's having a hard time and I had to call Dr. Graves. He's with her now."

Anger blazed from Cliff's narrowed eyes. "You let a horse come before our appointment with Dr. Michaels?"

"Yes. I tried to tell you I didn't want to go.

That Molly was due to have her colt."

Cliff grabbed hold of Tracy, his face close to hers. "You listen to me! No horse is going to spoil this for me! You get dressed and be out here in ten minutes." He gave her a shake. "Do I make myself clear?"

Tracy, her green eyes blazing, pulled free from his hold. "And you listen to me, Dr. Sampson! I have no intention of going with you today or any day! My life is here in Centerville. You can do as you please about San Mateo. Just don't try to count me in!"

Chapter IX

Having delivered her speech, Tracy walked back to see how Molly was doing. She heard a car door slam and the screech of tires on gravel. Cliff would never speak to her again, but it was all his fault. She had told him time and again that she was happy here in Centerville and didn't want to leave.

Tracy didn't think she had been gone more than a few minutes, but when she returned, Dr. Graves was removing his rubber gloves. He was smiling in satisfaction.

"All Molly needed was a little help. She has a fine colt. I wouldn't be surprised to see him win top honors at the horse show in a couple of years."

Tracy's eyes were fixed on Molly nuzzling a crumpled brown form on the straw in front of her. She went to the mare and put her arms around her.

"You did it. You had your colt." Tears wetting her eyes, she turned to Dr. Graves. "I'm so glad that you were available. Molly means a lot to me."

"I understand. She should be fine now. However, I would keep a close watch for a few hours. If anything else unexpected develops, just give me a call."

Tracy walked with the veterinarian to his car. As she watched him drive away, she gave silent thanks that she had come home. What would have happened if she had changed at the clinic and gone on to San Mateo right from work? She shuddered at the thought.

After looking in on Molly again, Tracy went into the house. The phone was ringing. She let it ring again, wondering if it was Cliff. Deciding that he would have no reason to call, she picked up the receiver.

"Green Eyes? I called the clinic. Maria told me you had gone home to dress before going away for the weekend. I decided to chance catching you before you got away."

"Oh, Andy! Well, yes—I had planned on going to San Mateo."

"With Dr. Sampson?"

"Yes. He had set up an interview with Dr. Michaels. They're planning on hiring a nurse practitioner. Cliff wanted me to apply for the position."

"Then you are planning on going to San Mateo with him?"

Tracy took a deep breath. "No. We—we had a difference of opinion. I won't be leaving Centerville."

"I say! That's good news. What about this evening? I just got in, but there's nothing on the book for the rest of the day. I think I owe you a dinner."

"I'd really like to go with you, but I can't. I have to stay right here."

"What's the matter? Don't you feel well?"

"I feel great. It's Molly."

"Molly? Oh, your horse!"

"Yes. She just had her colt. I had to call Dr. Graves. I have to stay here to watch her."

"You sure? I'd planned a surprise for to-night."

"I love surprises. Even so, I do have to stay home and look after Molly. Maybe another time."

After a few minutes of idle chatter, they hung up. Until then Tracy didn't realize how disappointed she was. Andy would think she hadn't wanted to spend the evening with him. Oh, well, even if everything else was wrong, at least Molly and her colt were all right.

Tracy changed into jeans and a faded T-shirt, then ran back out to see how Molly was doing.

She entered the corral, carefully closing the gate, then moved toward the shelter. Molly whinnied softly.

"Molly girl, are you all . . ."

Whatever Tracy meant to say died on her

lips at the scene being enacted before her. The colt was struggling to stand, encouraged by gentle nudges from his mother. With great effort, he finally managed to get all four feet beneath him and stood up, only to have his legs buckle. With another soft whinny, the mare bent her head and nuzzled the colt. Tracy, swallowing a lump in her throat, backed softly away. She would come back later.

In the house she realized she was hungry. She was looking in the refrigerator, wondering what to fix for lunch, when a car pulled up in front. Glancing out the window, she blinked as though to clear her vision. It couldn't be Andy! It couldn't be—but it was. With a singing heart, she went outside to meet him.

"This is a surprise! You didn't say anything about coming to Centerville."

"You said you liked surprises."

"I do." Ruefully she glanced down at her attire. "Sometimes."

Grinning, Andy said, "Anyway, I'm here. What's the saying about the mountain coming to Mohammed if Mohammed can't come to the mountain? As long as you couldn't spend the evening with me, I'm here to share your vigil with Molly. How is she, by the way?"

Tracy looked at Andy with stars in her

eyes. How unlike Cliff he was! She took hold of his hand.

"Come. You can see for yourself. And just wait until you see the colt!"

Molly nickered a welcome. Or was she voicing her pride in her offspring? One look at the colt on his wobbly legs and Tracy fell to her knees, throwing her arms around his neck.

"Oh, Andy, isn't he beautiful?"

Andy's gaze rested on Tracy. "Beautiful," he agreed.

"Did you ever see anything so perfect?" Tracy asked. "Look how well proportioned he is, and the white star on his face."

"He is kind of a cute little fellow. What are you going to name him?"

"I don't know. What do you think would be a good name?"

"How about Julio—for July? This may be a date we want to remember."

"Julio." Tracy cocked her head thoughtfully. "Julio. That's different. I'll think about it."

Tracy hugged the colt again, then stood up and moved to Andy's side. With a faint nicker, the colt took a tentative step, looked to his mother for encouragement, then took another step. Tracy clapped her hands in delight. Soon the colt had reached his mother's side and butted his head against her flank.

"Dinnertime," Andy commented.

"It's rather marvelous, isn't it? Animal instinct, I mean. I'm so glad I decided to let Molly have a colt. This is a truly wonderful experience."

"Even though it kept you from going to San Mateo with your doctor?"

"Yes. Only, I should never have promised to go with Cliff in the first place. I'm happier here in Centerville than I've ever been. I enjoy having my own place, and especially having my own horse. I tried to tell Cliff I wouldn't leave."

"But you planned on getting married?"

"Cliff and I have worked together for four years. We've had a very good relationship. It seemed inevitable to me that we would spend our lives together."

"And—now?"

Tracy sighed. "Now I don't expect Cliff to ever speak to me again."

She felt Andy's burning gaze. "Does it matter a great deal to you?" he asked.

By now they were walking toward the house. Tracy gazed off toward the hills, wondering how to answer Andy. The truth was that it mattered—and it didn't matter.

"Marrying Cliff would have been wrong. For both of us. Our basic interests are too dissimilar."

Andy grabbed her in a bear hug.

"Green Eyes, am I glad to hear you say that! You don't know what a strain I've been under since that phone call from your doctor. Only, I'm glad he's not your doctor anymore!"

With his arms still around her, he pressed his lips to hers. How wonderful Andy's kiss was. As the sweetness of it seeped through her, Tracy's arms wound themselves around his neck.

It was minutes before they stopped kissing and Tracy rested her head on Andy's shoulder. His arms tightened their hold.

"I love you, Tracy."

She looked up to meet his ardent gaze.

"And I love you, Andy."

Oh, how different this feeling was from what she had felt for Cliff! Andy bent to kiss her again.

"This calls for a celebration. Since we can't go out on the town, we'll have to devise something special for right here."

Eyes twinkling, Tracy said, "We could work in my garden."

"Not a chance!"

"We could call in a few friends."

"I don't like that idea any better," Andy said.

"Then how about a picnic by the river?"

"Now that idea I like! Do you have a small charcoal grill so we can do steaks?"

"It's kind of old, but I think we can use it.

I'm afraid we'll have to go shopping. I'm short on supplies since I didn't expect to be home."

"No problem. I can run to the store if you don't want to leave."

"I'll look in on Molly again, then go with you. We shouldn't be gone long. Just give me ten minutes to change into something different."

"Why bother? Besides, you look great to me."

Tracy stood on tiptoe and kissed him. "Thanks, but I'd feel better in something more presentable. This is my gardening outfit."

Tracy ran upstairs and, true to her promise, was back in ten minutes dressed in smart white shorts, a soft pink top, and sandals. Andy whistled.

"I like this outfit better." He placed his hands on her shoulders and, bending his head, kissed her again. "You're beautiful, Green Eyes. I've never met a more beautiful girl. I want you to know that."

Choked by emotion, Tracy said, "And you, Mr. Carlton, I think you're handsome."

Grinning, Andy ran his hand through his red hair. "Not many people call me handsome. Not with this hair and my pug nose."

"Others don't see you through my eyes!"

Kissing her again, Andy chuckled. "Green

Eyes, you're adorable! Please never change."

They stopped by the corral to see Molly and found her watching over the sleeping colt. As far as Tracy could tell, everything seemed normal. She could go on the picnic and not have to worry.

Driving down the hill to the highway, Andy said, "You get a good view of Spencer Valley. Vineyards, sheep, the saw mill. And Centerville! I can see why a doctor might find this setting dull. There's not as much here even as in Kingsley."

At the grocery store Andy went to the meat counter to get the steaks while Tracy picked up several other items. She and Andy paid for their groceries and started out the door just as Mrs. Bentley entered. Her gaze moved from Tracy to Andy, then back. With a curt nod she passed on into the store.

"Who was that charming person?" Andy asked.

"Mrs. Bentley, one of the clinic board members. She and I aren't exactly friends."

"I gathered that. What did you come to blows over?"

"Clinic matters. Very trivial. She wanted a fancier waiting room. Fancy drapes and so forth."

"And you prevailed?"

"Of course! There were more important things we needed."

Back home Tracy started to make some po-
tato salad, then ran out to look at Molly.
Andy found the grill and put it and charcoal
in the car, then got an ice chest and put ice in
it. He took a bottle of ginger ale out of a bag
and looked at it.

"This reminds me—a French champagne
house has bought land near here and will
open their winery before too long. I'm anx-
ious to see how they make out."

"And I'm wondering what effect they will
have on my work. There will be more tourists, for one thing. I wish I knew what doctor
will come when Cliff leaves."

Andy looked up from settling the ginger
ale on the ice. "You'll miss him, won't you?"

"Yes, I will. We do work well together.
Whoever comes will probably be just out of
school and will want to make a lot of
changes."

Andy laughed. "And you wouldn't like
that!" Seeing the sparks appearing in Tracy's
eyes, he hastily added, "We all resist change.
Sylvia has come up with some suggestions
lately that leave me cold. Having a working
partner can create problems, no doubt about
that."

The phone rang. Tracy answered, then
handed the phone to Andy.

"Sylvia."

Frowning, Andy took the receiver and

muttered, "Now what's up?" Into the mouth-
piece, he said, "What is it, Sylvia? I told you I
wanted the rest of the day free."

Tracy could not hear Sylvia's response.

But Andy's words were loud enough.
"You what! Signed me with a movie company?... Mendocino? Oh! For camera work.
When do they start shooting?... They're already on location? What happened to the helicopter they were using? Why don't they wait
to get it repaired?... The pilot's in the hospital? The fog was really that bad? Yes, yes, of
course I want the assignment! It seems
rather late for today.... Oh. Yes, of course. Is
Tim there? Have him fly the Bell to me here.
He can drive my car back to Kingsley."

Hanging up, his face radiating excitement,
he turned to Tracy.

"I'm sorry as anything, Green Eyes, but
this is something I can't turn down." He gave
her an absentminded kiss. "I wonder what
the weather will be like in the morning."

Fear clutched at Tracy. "What is it, Andy?
What are you going to be doing? It's something dangerous, isn't it?"

"Dangerous? Oh, you mean because the
other helicopter crashed!"

The blood drained from Tracy's face. "How
—why—what happened that it crashed?"

"The fog rolled in suddenly." Andy
shrugged. "The pilot misjudged. A rotor hit

the water and the helicopter plunged into the ocean."

"Why was he flying that low?"

"He's on location with a movie company who are doing a movie about a fishing boat. They want me to take over in his place."

"What will you be doing?"

"Piloting the cameraman. That's why they want me right away. They'll remove the tripods from the other copter and secure them to my Bell. That way we'll be ready to shoot first thing in the morning."

"How badly was the pilot hurt?"

"He's not critical. Fractured ribs and a broken arm, Sylvia said. The cameraman came out with a few bruises. He was more concerned with saving his film!"

Andy paced restlessly while scanning the sky, watching and listening. As soon as he heard the drone overhead, he hurried to the meadow where Tim would land. Tracy stood by the fence with Molly. The horse seemed nervous but, soothed by Tracy's presence, remained quiet as the helicopter landed. Andy hurried to meet it, ducking under the still gyrating blades as the door opened and Tim stepped out.

The two pilots remained in conversation for several minutes. Then Andy climbed in the whirlybird and lifted into the air while Tim, eyes shaded, watched with Tracy. If only she didn't have such a feeling of apprehension!

She thought: *Andy, why did I let myself fall in love with you? I can't go through what I went through with Dad and Kevin! I can't!*

Chapter X

Still clutched by apprehension and fear,
Tracy moved about the kitchen in a daze. She
drained the potatoes and placed them in a
bowl in the refrigerator without making a
salad. She put the steaks in the freezer. As
she removed the ginger ale from the ice
chest, tears again began to flow. How thrilled
she had been when Andy told her he loved
her. How excited they had both been getting
ready for their celebration picnic. Now
maybe there wouldn't be a celebration—
ever.

Too restless to remain indoors, Tracy
changed back into her jeans and T-shirt, then
looked in on Molly. The colt was still sleeping, the mare standing nearby. Tracy rested
her head against the mare's neck.

"Molly girl, right now I'd like a long ride."
The horse snorted and shook her head. "Oh, I
know! We can't go for a run today. I'll have to
settle for a good workout in my garden."

On her knees working the earth around
the various plants, Tracy felt a peace settle

over her. Soon there would be so many new
flowers. All from the seeds Andy had given
her. A tender smile played about her lips.
Andy. How she loved him! Nothing must
happen to mar their love. No, having lost two
loved ones to air crashes, she surely could not
lose one a third time. God wasn't so cruel.

This feeling of assurance was shattered by
the evening news. A helicopter, during a
scene for a movie being filmed along the
rugged Mendocino coast, had flown too low.
One of the blades hit the water, and the helicopter had gone into the ocean. The pilot had
been rescued, but was in the hospital with
multiple injuries. Andy had told her all of
this, but hearing it on the radio brought it
more vividly to life. And he had gone to fly in
that pilot's place!

Tracy stayed awake most of that night.

The next morning, groggy from lack of
sleep, but knowing it would be useless to remain in bed, she got up and dressed. She
would put the coffee on to perk, then check on
Molly. After breakfast she would call Sylvia
to find out what she had heard from Andy.

After tending to Molly, Tracy started back
to the house. As she neared the door, she
heard the phone. What if that was Andy? She
began to run, terrified the phone would stop
ringing before she got there.

"Where were you?" an irritated voice demanded. "I was ready to hang up."

Cliff. Tracy felt her heart plummet as she fought to catch her breath.

"Well, can't you answer?"

"I'm sorry, Cliff. I was out with Molly."

"Still that horse! Quite an alibi, isn't she?"

"Molly? An alibi? I don't understand what you mean."

"You're not that dense! I had dinner with the Bentleys last evening."

"What's that got to do—Oh! She saw me at the grocery store."

"You and that redheaded flyer. All that talk about having to stay home because of a horse! I thought it was phony."

"Cliff, have I ever lied to you?"

"I certainly never caught you in a lie before."

"Well, I didn't lie this time either. Molly did have a difficult delivery. If I hadn't found her when I did and called Dr. Graves, I don't know what would have happened. Dr. Graves was the one who advised me to stay close by Molly."

"Then how did that helicopter pilot get into the picture?"

"He phoned to ask me to dinner. I told him I couldn't leave because of Molly. He had the afternoon free, so he drove over to, as he said, keep the vigil with me. Since I had planned on being away and hadn't done any shopping, we had to run to the store to get food for dinner."

"Oh. I'm sorry if I accused you wrongly. I was upset."

"I realize that, and I'm sorry things worked out the way they did." A thought struck Tracy. "By the way, what were you doing at the Bentleys'? Didn't you go to San Mateo?"

"Without you? I'd already had my interview. I phoned Dr. Michaels to tell him something had come up so that we couldn't keep the appointment."

"Was he upset?" Tracy asked.

There was a silence before Cliff said, "As a matter of fact, no. He wasn't there. He and his wife had flown to Seattle for the weekend."

"And he didn't even phone to cancel our appointment?"

Ignoring her question, Cliff demanded, "What about that pilot? I don't like him hanging around your place."

"And I don't like you listening to gossip from Mrs. Bentley!"

So saying, Tracy slammed down the receiver. How could she and Cliff have gotten to this point in their relationship after the years they had worked in harmony? Hadn't they really known each other? Or had their dedication to getting the clinic established given them a common bond that no longer existed? Things couldn't go on like this until Cliff left. It wouldn't be fair to their patients to let personal animosity in any way affect the care they needed.

Sighing deeply, Tracy dialed Cliff's number. The line was busy. She poured herself a cup of coffee, then tried again.

"Oh, it's you," he said when he heard her voice.

"I called to apologize. I'm a little jumpy today. I didn't get much sleep last night."

"Did you run into more trouble with your horse?"

"Oh, no. Molly and the colt are fine. It's just—did you hear about the helicopter that crashed into the ocean near Mendocino?"

"The one on location, making a movie? I heard about it. I just talked to Sylvia. She said Andy flew over yesterday to take that fellow's place."

Tracy swallowed convulsively, trying to clear her throat. "Did Sylvia say whether or not she had heard from Andy?"

"Only that, since they're on location with not much more to do, they'll work right through the weekend. Sylvia asked if I would like to drive to the coast and watch them film. We'll have dinner in Mendocino."

"That—that will be nice. And interesting. I've never seen a movie being made."

"Well, take it easy. I'll see you Monday

morning. We have a full schedule!"

By the time Tracy took her first sip of coffee, her mind was made up. If Cliff and Sylvia could drive to the coast to watch them filming, so could she. Hurriedly she drank a glass of orange juice, made herself a slice of toast, drank a second cup of coffee, then ran upstairs. Showering in record time, she dressed in pale-green pants and a white blouse.

When Tracy started her car, Molly came to the place by the fence where she usually stood to watch her drive away.

"Take good care of Julio," Tracy called. "I'll be home early."

She tried not to worry about Andy as she drove to the coast.

Shortly before reaching Mendocino, Tracy noticed cars parked at a lookout beside the highway. Some distance from the shore she could see a fishing fleet with a helicopter hovering overhead. That must be Andy.

Tracy got out of her car and walked to the edge of the embankment. As she watched, the helicopter dipped lower and lower, almost skimming the surface of the water. Tracy stifled a scream and covered her eyes. When she removed her hands, the whirlybird had lifted high enough to hover above the boats.

"They're using the helicopter as a camera platform," a bearded young man explained to

his girlfriend. "See how the pilot maneuvers
into position? He can fly up, down, straight
ahead, sideways, or backwards. That way
they can shoot from nearly any angle."

"Do you know what movie they're filming?" the young girl asked.

"Not really. Something about a guy who
has his own fishing boat." Putting binoculars
to his eyes, he added, "That helicopter pilot is
darned good! You heard about the one that
crashed yesterday, didn't you? I understand
the pilot is still in the hospital." He put his
binoculars away. "I guess that's it for now.
Dan told me they stop shooting right at noon
so everyone can eat lunch. We might just as
well go."

Tracy remained a few minutes longer, then
decided to drive to the airfield and be there
when Andy landed.

She entered the airport parking lot and
parked her car. The helicopter was already
on the ground. Where could Andy have disappeared to? She got out of her car just as he
emerged from the far side of the machine.
Another man, with a camera resting on his
shoulder, followed him. They headed toward
where Tracy was standing. Deep in conversation, they would have walked right by if she
hadn't called out. Startled, Andy spun
around.

"Tracy! What are you doing here?"

"Satisfying my curiosity. I've never seen a

movie being filmed. So . . . I drove over."

Chuckling, Andy bent down and kissed her. "I doubt if you'll see much action. But I'm glad to see you." He turned to the sturdy black-haired man beside him. "Mike, I'd like you to meet a very special girl, Tracy Nichols. She's a nurse practitioner at the Centerville Community Health Clinic."

Tracy held out her hand. "And you're a cameraman! It's nice to meet you."

They all began talking about the movie. Then Andy asked Tracy if she would drive them to the Seagull Restaurant in Mendocino.

They were seated by a young, smiling waitress.

"Are you with the film company?" she asked. "It's so exciting having them do a moving picture here! I can't wait to see it."

"That won't be for a while," Mike told her. "We still have a lot of work to do on it. Our sequences here are only a small part of the movie."

"That was too bad about the helicopter crashing. We get fog in July, all right, but not often as thick as yesterday."

"No, today's beautiful. Let's hope and pray it stays that way," Mike replied.

"If there is fog, you won't go out, will you, Andy?" Tracy asked, her voice tinged with fear.

"For heaven's sake, Tracy!" Andy growled,

his brown eyes flashing. "Stop worrying! If there's anything I can do without, it's having someone around who gets panic-stricken every time I go out on a job."

Chapter XI

Tracy, eyes downcast, voice stilled by the lump in her throat, felt the tense silence, but could do nothing to relieve it. Why had Andy lashed out at her like that instead of trying to understand her fears? She had been right from the beginning. She should never have let herself become emotionally involved with another flyer.

Resolutely raising her head, she swallowed hard, then forced a smile.

"I'm sorry. Your life is your own to live as you see fit. The risks you take are none of my concern."

"Really," Mike interjected, "you have little cause to worry. We work with helicopters a great deal. The accident yesterday was most unusual."

"I don't think Tracy understands that there is risk in any profession," Andy said. "Even that of nurse practitioner."

"But that's different! It's not physical risk to myself."

"Don't you risk getting sick? And what

115

about risk to your patients? They rely on your judgment."

"And my training! I'm well qualified to do my job."

Andy snapped, "And I'm not qualified to do my job?"

"Oh, Andy! Of course, you're qualified! It's only—oh, let's forget it." Forcing a weak smile, she asked Mike several questions about shooting films.

After lunch, when Tracy had driven the two men back to the airfield, Mike climbed out of the car and looked at the ocean.

"Still clear and sunny. I hope that fog bank stays where it is."

He hurried toward the helicopter while Andy remained near the car looking down at Tracy.

"Are you going to be around this evening?"

"No. I have to get home. Besides, it will be better if we don't see each other again."

"Now what brought that on? Of course, we'll see each other, Tracy. I expect to be tied up here through Monday. I'll call you."

"Please I'd rather you didn't call."

Andy gripped her shoulder. "Let's get this straight. I'll call."

"Hey, Andy! Let's get going! The boats with the actors have already gone out!" Mike shouted.

Bending down and putting his head

through the open window, Andy planted a firm kiss on Tracy's lips.

"I'll be seeing you!"

Tracy, lips compressed, watched Andy sprint to the waiting bird, climb in, and take his place at the controls. In seconds the helicopter was over her head, with Andy waving good-by.

Tracy remained where she was, lost in thought. Were her fears about flying abnormal? Was flying really safer than driving a car—as people kept insisting?

Starting her Toyota, she left the airfield and drove back to the point overlooking the ocean. She got out of the car and walked along a pathway to the cliff's edge. Fingers of fog swirled around her, making her fearful. Then the fog grew heavier—and Tracy wondered why she didn't hear the helicopter return to the airfield and land.

Finally she heard the sound of a helicopter motor heading for the airfield. That had to be Andy! He had turned around and was coming in. Thank heavens.

Running to her car, Tracy got in and headed back to the airfield. She wanted to be there to watch Andy land. And to know that he was safe. Her foot lifted from the gas pedal as she let the car slow to a crawl. She couldn't let Andy know how worried and frightened she had been. He would chide her even more. Maybe it would be better to drive on home and not let him know of her terror.

Tracy didn't realize she was slowing traffic until she glanced through her rearview mirror and saw a car pressing close, the driver obviously annoyed. Finally he passed her. Only then did Tracy recognize Cliff's car and the blonde with him. Cliff and Sylvia. They were going to the airfield. Well, she, too, would be there to greet Andy when he landed!

By the time Tracy reached the airport, Cliff had parked and Sylvia was hurrying toward the helicopter landing pad. Cliff turned to Tracy in surprise.

"You didn't tell me you were coming to Mendocino."

"Do I have to report all my movements to you? I decided I would like to watch a movie in the making, so I drove over."

"This fog—when did it roll in? Sylvia was sure she heard a helicopter and is upset that Andy was flying. All of her money is tied up in this operation. I told her she should get out of this business."

Was Sylvia's concern for Andy—or for the machine he was flying? Tracy wondered.

Aloud she said, "I've never seen fog move so fast! It was clear and sunny when Andy and Mike took off. Then suddenly there was all this mist. I couldn't believe it!"

"Hmmm—well, who can outguess the weather these days? The unusual and unexpected seems the rule of thumb."

By the time Tracy reached the landing pad, Andy was just touching down. He shut the engines off and waited for the blades to stop turning before opening the door and stepping out. Sylvia rushed to him and threw her arms around him. His eyes met Tracy's over Sylvia's head. Did she see a glint there? Tracy wondered. Was he displeased or pleased?

With both hands, Andy removed the arms entwined about his neck. He smiled reassurance at Sylvia, saying something in too low a voice to carry. Sylvia nodded, her eyes intent on Andy. Tracy felt her heart sink. Andy owed a debt of gratitude to his buddy's wife. Wouldn't that, in the long run, carry a great deal of weight? Especially if Andy was annoyed with her because of her supposedly unjustified fears.

Mike, the cameraman, came around from the other side of the helicopter.

"I guess that's it for today," he growled. "We'll be stuck here for another day at least. What's there to do in this town, anyway?"

"Have you visited the art studios?" Sylvia asked. "Also the gift and craft shops."

Mike said, "That's something my wife would like. But she's not with me. And fish-

ing's out. It looks like it's my motel and hours
of television."

"If you like stage plays, a Mendocino
drama group is doing *Fiddler on the Roof*,"
Sylvia said. "You could attend that this evening. The actors are supposed to be pretty
good. You might enjoy seeing them. Dr.
Sampson and I plan to attend."

Tracy met Andy's compelling look. He said,
"Tracy and I are also going to see *Fiddler on
the Roof*. Come along with us. That will beat
sitting in a motel watching TV."

"I'm not sure—I hadn't planned on staying
so late," Tracy objected.

Andy's eyebrows rose. "I thought you didn't
mind driving at night. If you're afraid, I'll
drive you home."

"Of course, I'm not afraid!"

"Then it's settled. Tracy, will you drive
Mike to his motel? I've got some tinkering to
do on the helicopter. You can come back for
me later."

"Do you need me?" Sylvia asked. "If not,
Cliff and I will be on our way."

"No, there's nothing for you to do," Andy
assured Sylvia. "Why don't we all meet for
dinner? That new place that opened out on
the point is supposed to be good."

Sylvia turned to the doctor, who had
strolled over to join them.

"Is that all right with you? Or do you have

some other place you'd like to eat?"

"No. That sounds great. Only, we'd better meet for dinner no later than seven if we want to be in time for the play."

Tracy looked at her watch. "It's almost three now," she said. Where had the day gone? "I'm wondering if I'll have time to drive home, then come back."

"Drive to Centerville, then come back?" Andy looked puzzled. "Why even consider such a thing?"

"Probably that horse of hers," Cliff said.

"Is that why you want to go home before the play?" Andy asked. Tracy nodded. "If you got home, you'd probably decide not to come back. Why not call a neighbor to check on Molly and the colt?"

Mockingly Cliff chided, "Tracy—trust someone else to look after her Molly? You have to be kidding!"

Tracy glared at Cliff. The way he was behaving, she would be glad to see him leave.

"I guess I could call the Thompsons. I'm sure Billy won't mind giving the mare some water and putting out some feed."

She would tell Billy where they were having dinner so he could contact her if necessary. Wryly she wondered if Cliff might be right about her concern for a horse. Molly had seemed perfectly fine when she left. She was foolish to worry so much. Still...

An arm slid around her shoulders as she started toward her car. "Green Eyes, don't let the doctor's needling upset you." Andy chuckled. "Jealousy can sour the best disposition."

"Cliff, jealous?"

"I'm no doctor, but I recognize the symptoms." He placed both hands on Tracy's shoulders and turned her to face him. "You did tell the doctor that you were not going to leave when he did, didn't you?"

"Yes. I blew up at him yesterday. Only..." Tracy frowned in concentration.

"Only what?"

"Cliff never takes what I say seriously! He thinks he can override me and that I'll still change my mind."

"Is that why he's courting Sylvia? To make you jealous?"

If that was true, then it must be a three-way game. She would bet any amount that Sylvia was encouraging Cliff only to make Andy jealous. Oh, dear, how involved human relationships could become.

Cliff and Sylvia drove away, leaving Tracy to wait for Mike. He went into the office to make a phone call. She watched Andy as he circled the helicopter. Then he opened the door and got in to check something inside. It struck her that he was as concerned about his Bell as she was about Molly.

Mike came out and loaded his camera in the car. "I guess I'll accept Andy's offer to have dinner and go to the theater with you. I don't feel like partying and that's what the others plan. A local artist has invited them to his place. You can drop me off at my motel, then pick me up in time for dinner."

While heading for Mike's motel, Tracy slowed down to permit a car to pull up ahead of her. Then she saw a speeding black sports car bearing down on her, almost hitting her. A second later the danger was over. But the fog was as thick as ever.

Mouth dry, hands white-knuckled, Tracy let her breath out with a shudder. What a near miss that had been! And she had been worried about Andy. Why, he was as safe in his helicopter in the air as she was in her car here on the ground. Andy was right. Life could not be lived without risk.

Chapter XII

With time on her hands, Tracy decided to do a little shopping in Mendocino. Or at least some window-shopping. She had plenty of time to meet Andy before going to dinner.

When she arrived back at the foggy airfield, Andy rushed out to meet her, his face drawn with anxiety.

"Where have you been?" he demanded. "I phoned Mike. He said you let him off some time ago and headed back here. I've been crazy with worry."

"I just drove around and did a little shopping. There was no reason for you to worry."

"I didn't like you driving in this fog!"

"Oh, Andy! I've driven in worse fog."

"You could at least have phoned. I've been ready to leave for an hour."

"I'm sorry. From what you said, I expected you to be busy until time to go to dinner." Standing on tiptoe and pulling his head down to reach her lips, she kissed him. "Anyway, now you can understand my fears for you."

His arms drew her close as his lips claimed hers.

"Ummmmm," he murmered, then abruptly loosened his hold and stepped back.

"It's not the same at all! Your fears for me are exaggerated."

"And your fears for me weren't? The only difference was that we exchanged roles. This time you were doing the waiting and worrying."

That was true, of course, but so was Andy's accusation that her fears for him when flying went much deeper. In the future she would practice being more rational about the dangers in flying. Then, too, it was natural for a man to be concerned about a woman driving, she supposed.

Tracy hurried into the rest room to comb her hair and apply fresh lipstick.

When she came out, she said, "If I had gone home, I could have changed into something more dressy."

Andy bent down to kiss her. "You look great. People here are mostly on vacation. Everyone will be in casual attire. Now let's pick Mike up."

The restaurant was on a wind-swept point overlooking the ocean. They were shown to the only vacant table. Looking out at the gray expanse of water, Tracy said, "You must have made reservations early to get a window table, Andy."

"Not me. Your doctor. Frankly, I didn't even think of reservations."

Yes, Cliff was methodical and did plan ahead. Traits she had appreciated while they were getting the clinic started. Why now did these same traits irritate her?

"I wish my wife was here with me," Mike said, staring gloomily out the window. "This job is jinxed. We should have finished filming and be home by now."

"Tomorrow should be sunny," Andy told him. "How much more camera work is there?"

"Including the retakes, about two days. I'm counting on getting out of here Monday afternoon."

"That's good. I've got another job coming up that I have to do myself. Monday will work out nicely," Andy said.

Cliff and Sylvia arrived. After a few minutes of general conversation, Mike entertained them with stories of unexpected happenings at movie studios and on location.

Andy countered with humorous accounts of his experiences in the army. Sylvia enhanced these stories with observations of her own. Tracy listened with amused enjoyment. Cliff looked bored, obviously relieved when dinner was served. But at least he enjoyed the food.

"An excellent meal," Mike declared. "Thank you for inviting me."

"Our pleasure," Andy assured him. "I hope you find the local theater as enjoyable."

They drove to the playhouse and took their seats just as the orchestra members filed in.

Mike looked around with interest. "Quite a turnout! Do they play to a full house every performance?"

"Usually," Tracy told him. "The players get wholehearted community support, and then tourists find the plays a treat."

This performance turned out to be a very special treat. Everybody loved the show.

When it was over, Mike said, "That was fantastic. Really fantastic. I'm going backstage to tell the actors they were great."

"Then Sylvia and I will leave you," Cliff said. "It's quite a drive home."

Tracy and Andy waited while Mike made his way through the crowd to the backstage dressing rooms. Several people stopped to speak to Tracy.

Andy raised an eyebrow. "You're a lady of importance! How come you never told me?"

"Oh, Andy! Of course I know quite a few people. I've lived around this area four years and we are a close-knit group—stretched out over some miles."

Mike returned and they walked to the car. They drove him back to his motel.

He kissed Tracy on the cheek. "You and Andy have been lifesavers. I hope you come to Hollywood sometime and let me return the favor."

Laughing, Tracy said, "Don't count on it! I don't care if I never see Southern California again."

Mike handed her a business card. "You may change your mind, so keep this."

Tracy put the card in her purse, then asked Andy where he was staying.

"At a bed-and-breakfast place out nearer the airport. Sylvia and I came for the weekend once and found it very comfortable."

Jealousy stabbed at Tracy. So Andy had been romancing Sylvia!

"Sylvia's mom was with us. She enjoyed it immensely."

Letting her breath out in a sigh of relief, Tracy glanced at Andy and met his teasing brown eyes, then drove to the place. It looked like a comfortable old house.

Instead of opening the car door to get out, Andy took Tracy in his arms and kissed her. Her arms stole around his neck. Her lips responded to his demanding kiss. Her heart pounding, her eyes glowing, Tracy pulled away so she could look into Andy's eyes. He was breathing fast, his face tender. Before she could say anything, his lips reclaimed hers.

Placing her hands on his chest, Tracy finally pulled free of his embrace. She could feel herself trembling.

"Please, Andy! I have to go. But it has been a lovely day."

"I hate to let you go. Are you sure you don't mind driving alone? Tomorrow's Sunday. Why not stay over and drive home in the morning?"

"I couldn't do that. I've got things I have to do. And I really don't mind driving alone."

Andy bent down to kiss her. "It seems we meet only to say good-by. One of these days things will be different." After another rather long, demanding kiss, he added, "You won't change your mind about staying?"

"Positively, no!" To make her refusal less harsh, Tracy ran her fingers along Andy's face, then gently kissed him. "I have a million things to do tomorrow. And there's Molly—"

Andy groaned. "I'm beginning to sympathize with your doctor. You devote too much time to that horse."

"Well, she is mine, and she does have to be taken care of. Now with the colt—anyway. I've never before asked Billy to look out for her. I want to make sure everything's O.K."

"You win," Andy said with a last kiss. "Drive carefully. I'll call you as soon as I get back to Kingsley."

For the first few miles Tracy had to drive slowly through the wispy fog. Later the fog lifted and moonlight bathed the world. With no other cars in sight, she relaxed and let her thoughts blend in with the beauty and serenity of the night.

Just remembering Andy's kisses sent shivers of pleasure through her. How soon would they be married? Nothing had been said of marriage, but Andy did love her, of that she was sure. But she knew very little about his private life, really. Only that he was trying hard to establish a helicopter business—with Sylvia as a partner. And Sylvia wanted Andy for herself. When the crunch came, which would win out? Love—or business?

Tracy was still deep in thought when, nearing the turnoff to her rancho, she became aware of the smell of smoke. Then she noticed a faint glow against the sky. A fire! Near her place. No! It looked as if it was her place!

Gripped by fear such as she had never known, she stepped on the gas pedal and raced ahead, skidding with a screech of tires.

Gulping sobs wracked her as she made the last turn and knew for a certainty it was her home—now only a glow of embers with licking flames leaping into the night. Two fire trucks were in the yard. She could see men with hoses shooting water into the blaze. Screeching to a stop, she jumped out of her car and ran, veering from the house toward the corral. Molly! She had to save Molly and the colt!

Strong arms grabbed her.

Fighting, struggling, she screamed, "Let me go! Molly! I have to get to Molly!"

The arms were bands of steel. "Molly's safe. So is her colt."

Tracy stopped struggling and looked up into a face smudged with smoke, a grim mouth and eyes blurred by tears. Recognition came slowly.

"Cliff!"

"I'm sorry, Tracy. I wouldn't have wished this on you for anything."

"How—how did you get here?"

"We came back this way so Sylvia could pick up her car. Before going to Mendocino, I had an emergency at the last minute, so she drove over here to meet me. When we drove by your place, I happened to glance up that way—and saw smoke. We turned off the road and arrived just as the house burst into flames. Sylvia raced to one of the neighbors who called the Forestry fire department. They were here in record time, followed by the Centerville fire truck."

"But Molly—what about her?"

"I ran to move her and the colt while Sylvia went to phone. The Thompsons took the horse and colt to their place. They're both safe."

Free of this worry, Tracy hurried toward the smoking ruins of her home. Cliff walked with her. Joe Sweeney, a volunteer fireman and a neighbor, came to meet them.

"I'm mighty sorry, Tracy. The house was ablaze when we arrived."

Tracy shook her head, tears rolling down her cheeks. "My house! My lovely little home." One look at the trampled yard and she sobbed, "And my garden! My flowers all destroyed."

The fireman looked even more abashed. "I really am sorry, Tracy. There wasn't much else we could do."

Tracy touched his arm. "I know. How— how did the fire start? Do you know?"

"Not yet. When it cools down, we'll be able to investigate the cause. How long were you gone?"

"I left ten-thirty, I think. If only I had stayed home!"

"Nonsense," Cliff said. "You might have been in bed. Then what would have happened?"

"The doctor's right, Tracy. I'd guess the fire was caused by faulty wiring. You might have been trapped and not been able to get out."

"But my house! My clothes! Everything! I have nothing left!"

"You have your life and your land."

"And me," Cliff added wryly.

In a daze, Tracy started toward the smoldering embers. Wasn't there anything she could do? How could this have happened?

Why had she gone to Mendocino? If she had been home, surely she would have been able to do something. She felt a firm hand on her arm.

"Don't go any closer," Joe told her. "It's still dangerous."

"But what am I to do? Where am I to go? I don't even have a place to sleep!"

"With all of your neighbors and friends here? Any one of them will be glad to take you home with them."

For the first time Tracy became aware of the people crowding around, many in hastily donned clothes, others still in robe and slippers. Hattie Thompson stepped forward.

"Tracy, come on home with me. We've got room and I'll loan you a nightgown."

Cliff put an arm around Tracy's shoulders. "Or you can go home with Sylvia. She's waiting to see what you want to do."

"That's kind of her, Cliff, and I appreciate her offer. But I'd rather be closer to home. Besides, I want to look in on Molly and Julio to make sure they're both all right. I'll accept Hattie's offer to spend the night with her."

"Whatever you think's best. I guess we'll go on then. Sylvia does have to drive on to Kingsley."

After voicing their concern and offering sympathy, the neighbors who had gathered slowly faded away, and the fire trucks left.

Tracy turned to Hattie. Billy stood beside his mother.

"Do you mind if I stay here alone for a few minutes? I'll be along shortly," Tracy said.

"Billy'll stay. He can walk home with you."

Tracy walked slowly around the blackened mound that had been her home. The acrid smell of smoke burned her nostrils. She could even taste it. She stopped at one point and reached down to pull a bedraggled flower out of the wet ground. She had looked at these plants only this morning. How healthy they had been, sturdy green shoots with blossoms beginning to form. Her second planting. All that work for nothing! Overcome with grief, she bowed her head and wept.

A warm hand took hold of her hand. "Tracy, please don't cry! I'll help you replant your garden. And you've still got Molly. And, say, that colt's the cutest little guy ever! I bet he'll grow up to be a special horse!"

Laughing and crying at the same time, Tracy threw her arms around the twelve-year-old boy at her side.

"Oh, Billy! You're a lifesaver! I lost nothing that can't be replaced. How I'll do it, I don't know—but I will rebuild my house and you can help me replant my garden!"

Chapter XIII

Tracy slept little that night and was up and dressed, in the same outfit she had worn the day before, when the odor of coffee drifted over to her. Moving silently down the stairs, she paused at the kitchen door and looked at her neighbor. Hattie Thompson had a pleasant, round face, short curly brown hair, and wore glasses. She was wearing a blue terry-cloth robe with matching slippers.

They had only recently moved in and Tracy had seen little of them, merely exchanging greetings and commenting on the weather. Except for Billy. He had stopped by a couple of times to see Molly, and once Tracy had let him ride the horse around the pasture. How kind they were to offer her shelter when she needed it so badly.

Sensing her presence, Hattie Thompson looked up and smiled. "Hi! I hope you were able to get some rest."

"If I didn't, it wasn't my bed! I was very comfortable and do appreciate you taking me in."

"We're neighbors, aren't we? I'm sorry we had to wait for something like this to bring us together. I appreciate you letting Billy ride your horse, and he was thrilled when you sked him to feed her. Because of my husband's job, it's taken us longer to settle in than we planned."

"Oh, yes! He has a computer and plans on operating his own financial consulting firm. Is that right?"

Hattie laughed. "News does travel! Yes, that's basically what Ken will do. Breaking away from the city isn't as easy as he thought it would be. However, we both want to live in a rural community and raise our children here. I'm sure things will all work out, even if we don't have the material things we've been used to."

Tracy looked around the pleasant kitchen. "You have a comfortable home. You should be very happy here."

"What about you?" Hattie stopped and bit her lip. "I suppose it's too early to ask you anything like that. I do hope you will stay with us for the time being."

"I plan on rebuilding. I have no idea how I'll manage, but I will. Billy has offered to help me replant my garden."

By now Tracy was seated at the table with a cup of coffee in front of her. She sipped it thoughtfully, wondering what to do first. This being Sunday, what could she do? The phone rang. Hattie answered, then handed it to Tracy.

"It's for you."

"Tracy?" Cliff. She should have known. "I couldn't sleep, worrying about you. Have you had breakfast yet?"

"Just coffee."

"Good. I want you to meet me at Jeanie's Cafe. We have things to discuss."

"What kind of things?"

"Your future, for one. I'd rather we discussed it in person. Can you be here in twenty minutes?"

"Make it forty. I haven't gone out to see about Molly yet."

"That horse again!"

"Cliff, there's something I don't understand. Feeling the way you do about Molly, why did you make such an effort to get her clear of the fire?"

"I'm not heartless! And I knew how much she meant to you."

Tracy hung up the phone, a puzzled frown on her face. Would she ever understand Dr. Clifford Sampson? What contradictions people were!

"I'm sorry you won't be here to have breakfast with us," Hattie said when Tracy explained the phone call. "Ken and the children should be back soon. He took them to early Mass."

"Did I keep you home?" Tracy asked.

"Not really. I was glad to have a morning to myself. You will be here to have dinner with us, won't you? The family will be disappointed if you're not."

After promising to return, Tracy checked on Molly and her colt, then drove into Centerville. Cliff was really pushing things. And why was her future still of interest to him? He knew she didn't plan on spending it with him.

She found out, however, that Cliff didn't know any such thing.

"Just give up any idea of rebuilding," he told her. "I'm confident your house burned for a purpose."

Stunned, Tracy whispered, "Arson!" Her voice rose. "Someone deliberately started the fire! Is that what you mean?"

"No, that isn't what I mean. It was fate. Your house burning is proof to me that you aren't meant to stay here, but that you are meant to leave when I leave. We will go together just as I've always planned. I'll set up another appointment with Dr. Michaels."

"But, Cliff—"

Carefully buttering his toast, Cliff snapped, "And don't count on getting anywhere with that helicopter pilot. He's told Sylvia he has no interest in marriage. Not that he's in any financial position to take on family responsibilities. He recently took out a loan for another helicopter, and Sylvia signed the papers with him. She's already told me that if he becomes seriously involved with any other woman, she's pulling out."

Tracy had to bite her tongue to keep from blurting out, "But Andy loves me!" Hadn't she realized what a hold Sylvia had on him? With this new financial transaction, she would have a stranglehold.

They left the restaurant with nothing solved. Everything was exactly the same as when they had entered.

"I'll phone Dr. Michaels tomorrow," Cliff said as he walked Tracy to her car.

Tracy pressed her lips firmly together but said nothing. What good would it do? Cliff believed what he wanted to believe.

"What are your plans for today?" he asked. "It's too bad I have plans I can't change. I hate to leave you alone. Before you always had things to do at home. I don't suppose they've found out what caused the fire, have they? Have you phoned your insurance agent?"

"Today is Sunday. Anyway, by tomorrow I should have a report from the fire chief." She climbed into her car. "Right now I'm driving to Kingsley to buy a toothbrush, toothpaste, pajamas and something to wear to work on Monday. I promised Hattie I would be back for dinner with them."

"In that case, I'll run along. Just one thing more—be sure to keep next weekend free. I'm sure Dr. Michaels will want to meet and talk to you." He leaned through the open car window to kiss her. "I'm sorry about the fire, Tracy, but things will work out for the best. You'll see!"

Tracy had turned her head when she drove by her place on her way to meet Cliff. Now she drove back to see the ruins by daylight. There wasn't even part of a wall left standing. Everything had been destroyed.

She drove to Kingsley, did her shopping, and returned shortly after noon. Billy and his little sister ran out to meet her.

"We've been watching your colt for you," the little girl informed Tracy.

"And Molly, too," Billy added. "I bet she'd like to have someone ride her."

Chuckling, Tracy said, "And you would like to ride her!"

"Me, too!" his sister piped up. "Billy's ridden her and I haven't."

"Well, we'll have to remedy that. Let me change into jeans. Then we'll see about saddling her for a ride."

She was walking toward the house with the children, all laden with packages, when she heard the familiar drone in the sky.

"That's a helicopter up there," Billy said.

The helicopter circled, then began a descent directly toward them. "Hey, he's going to land here!"

Hands pressed over her pounding heart, Tracy watched the copter land. As the door opened and Andy stepped out, she broke into a run. His arms were open. She flew into them and buried her face against his shoulder. He held her close, his lips pressed to her hair. After a moment she raised her head.

"Darling, you shouldn't have left your job."

Andy's arms tightened around her. "Hang my job! I had to make sure you're O.K. I didn't hear until we came in for lunch. I would have been here sooner otherwise."

Billy and his little sister were staring at them in wide-eyed wonder. Hattie and her husband had also come out to see this unusual occurrence. Tracy introduced Andy to them.

"I'm glad Tracy has such kind neighbors. It's great of you to take her in," Andy said.

"We're pleased that she came to us. Besides, that's what neighbors are for."

"Do they know how the fire started?" Andy asked.

"They don't know for sure. One of the firemen said they thought it was faulty wiring," Tracy explained.

"We're grateful the fire was noticed soon

enough to get the fire fighters here in time to
keep it from spreading," Ken Thompson said.
"This has been an exceptionally dry year. We
could all have lost our homes."

Tracy shuddered at the thought. It was bad
enough for her to lose her home. She would
have felt awful had others suffered, too.

"Are you going over to see the burned
house?" Billy asked Andy.

"I saw it from the air when I flew over. It
looks like a total loss."

Tears slowly boiled up and spilled down
Tracy's face. Andy took her in his arms. Hattie quietly herded her husband and the children back to the house.

"Green Eyes, don't cry. The main thing is
that you're safe and, I understand, you have
the good doctor to thank for getting Molly
and her colt to safety."

"I—I know, and I am grateful. Only, my
very own home! It meant so much to me."

"I suppose it's too early to ask your plans."

"I'm going to rebuild! On exactly the same
spot."

"Sylvia says your doctor sees the fire as
fate—on his behalf. She says he feels you'll
have to leave now."

"I know! Mother feels the same way. I
called her this morning. They can't understand why I want to remain here in Centerville."

"Do you have to stay in Centerville? How about selling the land and moving to Kingsley?"

"Give up Molly and my garden? Not to mention my work at the clinic. No, my life is here. I've put too much of myself into it to give up now."

"Well, there's time to discuss it later. I've got to get back. How will you manage for now?"

"Hattie and Ken want me to stay with them for the present. I'll have to make more permanent arrangements in a few days. Rental units are scarce here in Centerville. I may put up a tent!"

"If only we could get married! Anyway, you wouldn't want to share my quarters. Maybe in a year or so things will be different."

With a fervent kiss, Andy climbed back in the helicopter, adjusted a few levers, gave a jaunty wave, then lifted off the ground. Eyes shaded, Tracy watched until the helicopter became a speck in the sky. She veered from disappointment and chagrin over the casual way he had brushed aside any thought of marriage to joyous elation that he had cared enough to take time off from the job to come and see that she was all right.

Flying to see her was a flamboyant gesture, typical of the redheaded pilot, but an extravagance he should have foregone. Still, she loved him all the more for coming. Even though Cliff had been right. Andy was too indebted to Sylvia to commit himself to anyone else.

Tracy went to work Monday morning glad that the day would be so filled that she would not have any time to worry about personal problems.

The first patient to arrive was an elderly woman, a diabetic, brought in by a neighbor.

The neighbor said, "I stopped by to see Mrs. Murphy this morning since I hadn't seen her around at all yesterday. She looks sick to me."

The patient did look extremely ill. Her skin was dry, her face flushed and feverish, her breathing rapid and shallow, her pulse weak. Tracy took her to a treatment room, had her lie down, and covered her with a blanket.

"When did you have your last insulin?" she asked.

"Friday, I think." Her words came out thick because of the dryness of her mouth. Her eyes were closed.

Having gotten the patient's chart and checked the insulin dosage, Tracy began filling a syringe from a bottle.

"You know better than to miss your medicine. You could have gone into a coma."

The woman opened her eyes, gave a feeble

nod, then closed them.

After administering the insulin, Tracy started intravenous fluids. When Cliff arrived, they would decide whether or not to send her to a hospital.

"How did you let yourself get out of insulin?" Tracy asked.

"I had no one to take me to get my prescription refilled. You know I don't drive anymore."

"You should have called someone. You do have neighbors."

"Who wants to bother with an old lady like me? It's not easy when you're old and alone and live in the country. In a city I could go on a bus and not bother others."

It was true. Older people living alone in rural areas did have greater problems getting medical attention than those living in a city. That had been a point in helping to establish the need for the clinic.

Watching as Mrs. Murphy's breathing became normal and her pulse grew strong and even, Tracy felt a glow of accomplishment. The time and effort she had given to the clinic had been well invested. She couldn't leave now. There was still too great a need. Why couldn't Cliff see that?

Her next challenge would be to rebuild her house. It would not be easy. Sighing heavily, she rechecked the I.V. and made sure Mrs.

Murphy was comfortable. Then she went into the next room where a young mother waited with a sick baby.

Chapter XIV

Late that afternoon the fire chief stopped by the clinic.

"We've checked everything out. As far as we can determine, faulty electrical wiring caused the fire. I'm sorry about your loss, Miss Nichols. However, it's a blessing the fire was contained as quickly as it was. This area's a tinderbox due to such a dry winter. We would have had a disaster on our hands if the fire had spread."

"I realize that. It's fortunate Dr. Sampson noticed the smoke and went to investigate."

"It certainly was. By the way, how did he happen by just at that crucial time?"

"Fate, he says. Dr. Sampson, Sylvia Duncan, Andy Carlton, and I had dinner together in Mendocino, then went to see *Fiddler on the Roof*. Before going to Mendocino, Dr. Sampson had a last-minute emergency, so Sylvia drove from Kingsley to meet him here. They left the play and came directly to Centerville. Andy is on a job at Mendocino, so I drove him to the place where he's staying. Then I drove on home."

"Andy Carlton, that redheaded pilot? He runs Carlton Helicopters, doesn't he? Used to be Kingsley Helicopters."

"Yes. Anyway, Cliff knew I wasn't home. So when he noticed smoke coming from what he thought might be my place, he went to investigate."

"And a good thing he did! Everybody else was in bed and wouldn't have noticed the fire until flames lit the sky. You owe that doctor a debt of gratitude."

She did owe Cliff a debt of gratitude, she reminded herself. Had the fire and his being the one to discover it been mere chance, or was Cliff right—and did his being at that place at that particular time have some special significance? If so, did that obligate her to comply with his wishes?

Fortunately Tracy did have fire insurance. Unfortunately the house had not been fully paid for. It might be some time before she could save enough money to even consider rebuilding. Maybe she would end up living in a tent!

Andy phoned Monday evening to tell Tracy he had completed his job with the movie company but had to leave early Tuesday for a job with the power company, stringing a power line in a remote mountain area, so he wouldn't be able to see her. He might be gone one week. It could be two.

"I had hoped we could have our picnic by the river," he said. "We still haven't celebrated."

"We had dinner and went to the theater. Wasn't that a celebration?"

"Not exactly what I had in mind. Not that I didn't enjoy the evening! I did. It's just that you and I haven't had any time alone. Your doctor has an edge on me. He sees you every day."

"Why do you persist in calling Cliff my doctor?"

Chuckling, Andy said, "Well, isn't he? At least if you want him, he's yours."

Caustically Tracy replied, "I didn't realize you had joined the conspiracy."

"Conspiracy? What conspiracy?"

"Needling me into a feeling of guilt where Cliff's concerned. Even the fire chief reminded me of the gratitude I owe him. And Mom! She's gone so far as to set a date for our wedding!"

"Now, Green Eyes, you know I was teasing. I love you. You can't doubt that. Maybe I'm envious of your close relationship."

"But I explained that! Anyway, what about you and Sylvia?"

"Ours is strictly a business partnership."

"On your part, maybe."

"That's ridiculous. Sylvia will never love anyone the way she loved Jim. They were one happy couple."

Was Andy really that blind? No wonder
Sylvia felt frustrated! And what would happen if the scales fell off Andy's eyes?

"Will you be away until you complete the
job with the power company?" Tracy asked.

"Unless something unexpected comes up.
I'll phone, though, to see how you're doing.
Just hang in there! Things will work out."

Tracy did hang in there for the rest of the
week. Ken Thompson went to San Francisco
for several days, so Tracy remained with
Hattie and the children. She put Molly and
the colt back in their own corral.

Billy had adopted the horse and colt and
went by to see them at least once a day.
When Tracy had time, she saddled the horse
and let both children have a ride. By now the
colt had gained enough strength to frolic in
the pasture, and each evening waited at the
fence with his mother for Tracy to come
home.

On Wednesday Cliff asked Tracy to see him
in his office.

"I've been accepted and will become a family practitioner at the clinic in San Mateo,"
he informed her. "Dr. Michaels still hasn't
found a nurse practitioner. I've practically
secured the job for you since you will be
working directly with me. There is no way
you will be able to rebuild your house. Con-

struction costs themselves are prohibitive. We can keep the land. Taxes won't be that high. In a few years we can build a second home and you can get another horse."

Eyes smoldering, Tracy said, "And Molly? What happens to her?"

Cliff looked surprised. "Sell her, of course! Maybe the Thompsons will buy her." Ignoring the fire in Tracy's green eyes, he continued, "We're due in San Mateo on September first. I've mailed in my resignation and requested a replacement. I want you to do the same."

Mouth open to protest, Tracy stared at Cliff, speechless. He honestly thought he was in the right and that she would submit to his high-handed tactics. What gave him such assurance? Biting back a scathing reply, she forced herself to speak calmly.

"Just why are you so sure you're right in this matter, and that I will meekly follow?"

"First, because I want you with me. I've loved you very much. Somehow we never got around to that. But I assumed you knew I loved you just as I always knew you loved me. The fire cinched things as far as I'm concerned. It could have been for no purpose other than to convince you."

Tracy didn't know what she would have replied if Hazel Connors hadn't knocked on the door and told her an obstetrical patient was

there, and it looked as if she might be starting labor.

"And I don't suppose you want the baby
born here!" Hazel added.

Tracy had been seeing the woman for her
prenatal care and knew it was her first child.

"You've made arrangements at Kingsley
Community Hospital, haven't you?" Tracy
asked.

"Yes," the woman replied. "I wanted you to
make the decision about calling my husband
away from work. We need the money and I
didn't want to call him if it was a false
alarm."

"How did you get here?"

"A friend brought me."

"I'm sure you're starting labor. I'll phone to
have your husband pick you up here. You
should leave immediately for Kingsley."

"I won't have the baby on the way?"

"No. The baby won't be ready to come for
two or three hours at the least. I'll phone the
hospital so they will be expecting you."

The husband arrived within minutes, and
Tracy saw them on their way. Maybe someday the clinic would handle deliveries, but
for the time being they would utilize the facilities at Kingsley. At least the young
mother could return to Tracy for postnatal
care, and she would see to the care of the
baby.

With this on her mind, she didn't have
time to think about her talk with Cliff until
she stopped by to see Molly on her way home.
The stark reality of her loss stared at her
from the mound of ashes that used to be a
house.

Rebuilding would be a major task, and
where would she get enough money? Even if
she started with one or two rooms and added
more later, it would take more money than
she could scrape up. It wasn't only the house
—everything in it. Tracy had already spent
quite a bit on clothing and grooming essen-
tials. Dishes, cooking pots, furniture—everything she owned was gone. Her books, her
stereo—all the things her father had given
her—all her mementos—all gone, all burned
in the fire.

She would command a higher salary if she
went to San Mateo. Maybe she should change
her mind and go with Cliff. She did owe him
a debt of gratitude. And he and Mom could
be right about the fire. She could be meant
to spend her life with Cliff instead of Andy.
But, oh, how hard it would be to give Andy
up!

When she hadn't heard from him by Friday, she decided he had been too busy and
couldn't phone. However, when both Saturday and Sunday passed without any word,
Tracy became alarmed. She tried reaching

Sylvia by phone, but there was no answer. She wondered about the gleam in Cliff's eyes when he appeared at her office door on Monday morning.

"Too bad about your redheaded helicopter pilot, isn't it?"

"Andy?" Tracy's heart leaped to her throat. "What do you mean? Has anything happened to him?"

"He was stringing a powerline over a mountain area and—"

"He crashed! Like Dad and Kevin, Andy crashed!"

Feeling terror building, Tracy sank into a chair, covered her face with her hands, and began to sob.

Hadn't she known this would happen?

She felt Cliff's hand on her shoulder and looked up into narrowed eyes.

"You're wasting your tears, you know. That pilot must lead a charmed life. Talk about a freak situation!"

Tracy grabbed Cliff's arm. "Tell me! What happened! Are you sure Andy is all right?"

"If he's not, Sylvia is there to hold his hand. She dashed off as soon as she heard about his brush with disaster."

"Brush with disaster? Tell me what happened!"

"It seems some bigwig in the power company came to check on the job he was on and ask Andy to fly him over a densely forested area. Visibility through the trees was poor, so Andy had to fly at treetop level. A sudden gust of wind threw the copter off balance, shearing off the top of one tree and tangling with another. Sylvia says no one but Andy could have managed to land with as little damage to the helicopter and none to himself or his passenger."

"Are you sure Andy's not hurt? How much damage was there to the helicopter? Will Andy be able to complete this job?"

"Actually Sylvia flew up with Tim. Andy wanted the other helicopter. He felt they could get the damaged one in condition to fly back to Kingsley where the mechanic can work on it. I tried to stop Sylvia from going. That helicopter may be all right for a pilot to risk his neck in, but not hers."

"Andy won't let her fly in an unsafe machine." With a speculative look, Tracy asked, "Why all of your concern for Sylvia?"

Cliff looked momentarily uncomfortable, then shrugged. "Sylvia and I are friends. We enjoy each other's company. It's only natural for me to be concerned for her welfare."

Sylvia, with her blond beauty and business acumen, was not only attractive but interesting to talk to. It wasn't surprising that Cliff found her entertaining. Was it her attachment to Andy that kept the friendship from blossoming into romance? If so, why was Cliff still pushing her, Tracy, to go away with him?

"When did all of this occur and how did you hear about it?" she asked.

"It happened late Friday afternoon. Sylvia phoned me Saturday morning. We—ahhh— had plans to have dinner together." Quickly he added, "Remember? You told me Hattie Thompson and her children had asked you to go to one of the state parks over on the coast to have a picnic."

"Why didn't you let me know about this sooner?"

"From what Sylvia said, no great damage was done. I thought you had enough to worry about right now."

Was that why Andy hadn't phoned? He hadn't wanted to worry her, either. But she had worried as much not hearing. How could one help worrying when one loved someone? What about the resolve she had made? Of course, she had known she couldn't completely banish concern and worry when Andy was flying. What she had resolved was not to become paranoid, and not to let Andy know of her concern.

Even so she wouldn't rest until she talked to him and knew for herself that he was all right. It would mean a phone call to Sylvia to get his number. She would have to wait until her lunch break. Sylvia would certainly be back at Kingsley by then.

"Oh, Andy's fine," Sylvia told Tracy when she finally reached her after several tries. "It means more expense to repair the helicopter, though. And Tim lost out on a job. Andy's not in a very happy frame of mind."

"I'd like to talk to him. Can you give me a phone number where I can reach him?"

"He'll probably go out to dinner. It may be late when he gets back to his room."

"Then I'll keep trying until I get him."

"I'm not sure it's wise for you to bother him. If he wants to talk to you, he'll phone."

In a determined voice, Tracy said, "Sylvia, I want to call Andy. Will you please give me the number where I can reach him?"

It took several calls before Andy answered.

"Tracy! I was thinking about calling you."

"I've been wondering why you didn't call. You should have told me about your accident."

"It was nothing! Just a little mishap. It was enough having Sylvia upset. I saw no reason to concern you."

"But, Andy, I love you! Of course, I'm concerned about what happens to you!"

"How are things going with you?" he asked. "Are you still at the Thompsons'?"

"Yes. It doesn't look like I'll be able to rebuild. I had no idea what the total cost would be."

"Don't I know! I had wanted to add a third

helicopter. Now it looks like I'll have to put that off until I accumulate more money."

"I may have to do the same. I really would make more money by going to San Mateo to continue working with Cliff."

Tracy waited for Andy to protest. After a strained silence, he said, "Maybe that would be best. Heaven knows my situation hasn't improved. I'm lucky to still be in business. Sylvia—"

Tracy almost heard him clamp his mouth shut. What pressure was Sylvia putting on him? Had she torn the scales from his eyes? Did Andy know Sylvia was in love with him? Would knowing that make him feel a greater obligation? Then where did that leave her?

In a shaking voice, Tracy asked, "When will you be home?"

"Probably a few days. We should finish up here by then. I'll be in touch."

Tracy slowly replaced the receiver, almost sorry she had phoned. No wonder Sylvia had discouraged her. Sylvia had disclosed her motives and put Andy on the spot. Still, Andy had extricated himself from sticky situations before. Now that he saw Sylvia not as his best friend's wife, but as his widow, who was in love with him...

Impatiently Tracy shook the thought from her mind. Andy loved her and she loved him. And love could surmount obstacles. If both parties loved enough! Then why was she even considering leaving Centerville to work with Cliff—maybe marry him? And why did she fear that Andy would give her up rather than chance losing Sylvia as a business partner?

Distracted with concern for Andy and with her own problems, Tracy went through the next two days in kind of a trance. She performed her job, but at the Thompson home she took little part in family conversations and made excuses when Billy wanted to ride Molly. Wednesday evening Billy extracted a promise from her that he could have a horseback ride the following day. The promise slipped her mind when Mrs. Bentley phoned and asked her to stop by her house on her way home.

Mystified, Tracy promised to be there. But why would Mrs. Bentley want to see her? They had hardly been on speaking terms since the clinic opened.

Mrs. Bentley lived in a neat white frame cottage on Main Street. She came to the door before Tracy knocked.

"Thank you for stopping by," she said, leading Tracy to a table set for tea. She motioned her guest to sit down, took her own chair, and asked, "Do you like anything in your tea?"

"No, just plain."

Handing Tracy her steaming cup, Mrs.

Bentley said, "We were all distressed at your loss. A fire is such a disastrous occurrence. I hear you're still with the Thompsons."

"Yes. They've been great. But I can't impose on them much longer."

"Dr. Sampson tells me he'll be leaving us at the end of August. I guess we rather expected that he wouldn't renew his contract. However, he tells me you will be leaving with him. Is this true?"

"I hadn't planned on leaving. Now—I don't know."

"Is the loss of your home your reason for leaving Centerville?"

"That will certainly influence me. At present I see no way to rebuild."

Nothing more was said on this subject. Tracy drank her tea. They discussed a few topics which would come up at the next board meeting. Then Tracy left.

Had she noticed a gleam of satisfaction in Mrs. Bentley's eyes? Would the woman be glad to see her leave? Had she been scouting around and found someone to replace her?

With a bitter laugh, Tracy wondered if the decision to remain in Centerville or to leave might be taken from her hands. Maybe Cliff was right. A force stronger than herself was shaping her future.

Chapter XV

As she turned off the highway, Tracy remembered her promise to Billy. Would he still be waiting? Why hadn't she remembered in time to phone? She really hadn't meant to disappoint him. Well, there would still be time for a short ride. She would make it up to him later.

Molly wasn't at the fence waiting. The colt trotted to the fence alone. Where could Molly be? She was not in her shelter—but the saddle was gone! And the bridle. Had Billy saddled Molly and gone riding by himself? If he had, it was her fault for not being here as she had promised.

Certain that he had ridden home to let his sister have a ride, Tracy got back in her car for the short drive. Little Gina ran to meet her.

The child asked, "Where's Billy? He's supposed to be home by now. Dinner's all ready."

"Why, hasn't he been here? I thought he must have ridden Molly home so you could have a ride."

"He's stingy! He doesn't want me to ride Molly!"

If Billy wasn't here, where could he be? Tracy wondered, walking back to the road to look for a boy on a horse. The road was empty as far as she could see. Where had Billy disappeared to? He wouldn't venture off the road, would he?

Worried, Tracy went into the house, Gina at her side.

"Mama, Billy saddled Molly and rode off all by himself!" Gina called out in an excited voice.

Hattie turned to Tracy. "Billy wouldn't do that, would he? He said he was meeting you."

Feeling guilty, Tracy nodded. "He expected to meet me. I did promise. Then Mrs. Bentley asked me to stop by to see her, and I forgot. I should have phoned."

"But Billy's never ridden Molly unless you were there, has he?"

"Oh, yes, he has! One time, but he told me not to tell."

"Billy rides very well. And I did show him how to saddle up. He must have gone for a canter up the road. He may have ridden further than he intended to ride."

"Or else he went into the hills. Billy told me that someday he was going to explore clear to the top of that hill we can see from the yard," Tracy said.

"But not today! Not all by himself," Hattie protested.

"I'll drive back to my place. He's probably there by now," Tracy said.

Only, Billy wasn't there. Just Julio, nickering in a whimper, running in circles, missing his mother. Tracy tried to soothe the colt, but that didn't appease his hunger!

She waited fifteen minutes, then decided to go looking for Billy. Hattie would have gone with her, but they decided it would be better for her to wait by the phone.

Tracy followed the road to where it ended. There was no sign of a boy or a horse. She stopped at several houses. Finally one man told Tracy he had seen a boy on horseback turn off the road and ride toward the hills. He hadn't seen him return.

The sun had gone down in a blaze of rose and flame, and dusk had settled over the valley by the time Tracy gave up her hunt. How could she face Hattie? Still, there was nothing more she could do. They would have to call the sheriff and send out a search party on foot. A boy and a horse shouldn't be that hard to find!

The sheriff had arrived and several neighbors had volunteered to help with the search when Tracy heard galloping hoofbeats along the dark road.

"That must be Billy!" she cried, breaking

into a run. One glance told her the approaching horse was riderless and running as though pursued. She leaped into the center of the road, arms outflung.

"Molly! Molly girl!"

The horse barely slowed and would have veered to pass, but Tracy grabbed hold of the dangling bridle. Flinging her head, shying in fright, Molly pulled Tracy several feet before she could bring her to a stop.

Hattie arrived at her side. "Billy! What's happened to Billy?"

By now they were surrounded by Sheriff Reeves and four neighbors who had responded to his call for volunteers.

"Does the horse seem to be O.K.?" Sheriff Reeves asked.

"Just frightened, as far as I can tell," Tracy answered.

"The boy must have fallen off. Well, we'd better get going. He may be hurt."

Face drawn with grief, eyes swollen from crying, Hattie disappeared into the house to place a call to Ken while Tracy unsaddled Molly and turned her into the pasture. Nickering in joy, the colt ran to meet her. Watching mother and colt nuzzle each other, Tracy's heart almost broke as she realized what this must be doing to Hattie. And Billy being lost was all her fault. She should have been here at the time she promised.

Ken arrived from San Francisco shortly after midnight. He insisted on joining the search.

"If Billy's out there, I'll find him," he said.

Gina refused to go to bed so her mother let her sleep on the sofa. Tracy kept a pot of coffee hot. They consumed cup after cup. If only there was something she could do to help! What if they did find Billy and he had a broken leg or worse?

How would they get him to a hospital? Suddenly her face lit up with joy. Andy! She would call Andy and they would join the search by helicopter!

A sleepy voice answered.

"My heavens, Tracy, this is the middle of the night!"

"Not when you haven't been to bed. Andy, I need your help. Billy Thompson rode off on Molly yesterday afternoon. Molly came home without him. They've been hunting all night. It's my fault he's lost. I'm afraid he's injured. Can you pick me up in your helicopter and join the search from the air?"

"Let's see—it's after four now. Dawn can't be too far away. Say forty minutes or so— how's that?"

"Oh, Andy, I do love you! I'll be watching for you!"

By the time Andy arrived, Tracy was pacing the yard, an impatient eye on the sky.

Hattie watched from the porch as Tracy climbed in beside Andy.

"We'll bring Billy back," Tracy called to her.

"Sorry I'm late," Andy apologized. "I had to put a stretcher in and check the first-aid supplies."

"You don't know how much I appreciate you doing this. I feel terrible about Billy."

"Well, rescue work is part of my job. And don't blame yourself. Billy knew better than to ride Molly without you being there."

By now they were flying well above the trees. Looking down, Tracy could see the hills, but no Billy. She kept her eyes peeled for signs of movement.

They had been circling for ten minutes when Tracy, pointing, called out, "There! Someone's down there waving at us!"

Andy flew lower. On the ground a man was waving his arms and running. Tracy couldn't contain her excitement.

"Do you think they've found Billy?"

"There's a clear spot there. I'll land and find out."

Tense and apprehensive, Tracy watched the ground come up to meet them, then felt the impact as they touched land. She had her door open and was on the ground when Ken arrived, breathless and disheveled.

"Thank heavens! We found Billy. He got

thrown and is hurt. It's his leg. Also, he's got a bump on his head. The sheriff was just leaving to arrange transportation for Billy. You're the answer to a prayer."

Andy helped remove the stretcher and carry it to where Billy lay on the dry grass. He was covered with a jacket, his right leg stiff in an improvised splint. He looked up at Tracy, tears in his eyes.

"I'm sorry, Tracy."

She leaned down and kissed his cheek. "I'm the one who should be sorry. I promised to be there so you could ride, and I wasn't."

"Molly—Dad said she got home. Is she O.K.?"

"She's fine. But what happened? How did she throw you?"

"I—I got lost. Molly wouldn't always go where I wanted her to go. But it was that old buck deer! He jumped out of a bush and scared Molly. She reared back and—I fell off."

While they were talking, Tracy checked the lump on Billy's head, looked at his eyes, felt his pulse, then turned to the sheriff.

"There might be a slight concussion. Since you've already splinted Billy's leg, we can move him onto the stretcher."

"You don't want to resplint the leg?"

"No. I'd rather not disturb it, but I will reinforce it with an ace bandage."

They moved Billy, Tracy supporting the injured leg while the sheriff and his father lifted him onto the stretcher, then carried him to the waiting helicopter.

"Does Hattie know Billy's been found?" Tracy asked.

"Yes," Ken replied. "The sheriff relayed the message through one of the search party."

"Where do you want Billy taken?" Andy asked after checking to see that the stretcher was securely in place. "To the clinic—or to Kingsley to the hospital?"

"The clinic would be handier," Ken said.

"No," Tracy replied. "Let's take him directly to the hospital. If it's the femur, he may need a pin inserted. You can radio ahead for a doctor, can't you?" she asked Andy.

"Of course." He looked at Ken. "I suppose you'll fly with us?"

"If there's room. Hattie will meet us there."

The excitement of riding in a helicopter soon wore off and Billy drifted off to sleep. Tracy held one hand as she brushed his hair off his forehead with the other. The circles around his eyes gave evidence of his ordeal. What a long, lonely night it had been! Yet how bravely he had faced it.

After seeing Billy safely in Emergency with his father still at his side, Tracy flew to the airfield with Andy. He covered her hand with his.

"Green Eyes, we sure do meet under the most difficult of circumstances. It would be nice if we could stay in the air and continue on to some deserted island. I never see you alone!"

"You don't know how much I appreciate your help with Billy. That means so much to me."

With raised eyebrows, Andy said, "More than spending time alone with me?"

"You know better than that! I'm free this weekend. What are your plans?"

"Some real estate developer wants me to fly potential clients over land he's trying to sell. You know the deal—give them a fancy meal, let them see the land from the air, then give them the hard sell. The money's too good to turn down." He gave her a side glance. "I don't suppose you could play hooky today?"

"I'd like to. But there's no way." She glanced at her watch. "My first appointment is scheduled for nine. And I have to find a way back to Centerville!"

"Promise to have breakfast with me. Then I'll drive you. I'm free until eleven. I have an appointment at the bank then."

And Sylvia will keep that appointment with you, Tracy told herself. She was clearly in the picture. Even so, breakfast with Andy was better than nothing.

Tracy hadn't realized how hungry she was

until the waitress brought her ham, eggs, hash brown potatoes, and toast. Only then did she remember she had not eaten dinner, and had been up all night. This was going to be a long day.

On the drive to Centerville, Tracy rested her head on Andy's shoulder and slept. He awakened her with a kiss. She opened her eyes and met his quizzical gaze.

"Oh, Andy! I'm so sorry! We didn't get to talk, did we?"

"No, but I enjoyed looking at you asleep." A sly grin spread across his face. "What thoughts I indulged in! And now all I can do is give you a chaste kiss and drive away."

Laughing, Tracy lifted her face, her lips pursed. The kiss she received was far from chaste. Breathless, her face flushed, she slid toward the car door and put her hand on the handle.

"When will I see you again?" she asked.

"I'll have to call you. Sylvia certainly keeps our schedule heavy. But I'm not complaining! She's much better at promoting business than I would be alone." As Tracy started to get out of the car, Andy said, "How are things working out for you? Have you any hope of rebuilding?"

"I see no way at present. Mrs. Bentley asked me by her house. Cliff told her I was leaving with him. You know we haven't seen eye to eye over clinic policy. I wouldn't be surprised if she isn't looking for someone to replace me. My hand may be forced."

"After all your work in starting the clinic! They wouldn't do that to you."

Tracy shrugged. "I wouldn't guarantee it."

"Well, something will work out. You'll manage."

With a flip "Thanks for your vote of confidence!" Tracy closed the car door and ran inside. Andy was giving her lukewarm support at best. He wasn't even discouraging her from going with Cliff! If he sincerely loved her, wouldn't he beg her to stay in Centerville? She sagged with defeat. Andy needed Sylvia. And that was that.

July passed and Spencer Valley basked beneath the August sun. With each passing day pressure on Tracy increased. She couldn't leave Centerville! This was home. Only, her home had burned and leaving might be the only way she could regain it.

D-Day came on the Monday the clinic board had its regular meeting. Tonight she would have to give her final answer.

Cliff arrived at work jovial and smiling. Tonight the board would announce his replacement. How smug he looked, Tracy fumed. There was no doubt in his mind about the outcome. As far as he was concerned, she was on her way to San Mateo.

Chapter XVI

The board meeting was held in the waiting room of the clinic. By seven-thirty that evening the five board members, plus Tracy and Cliff, had gathered around the table. Tracy had tried to read the expression on Mrs. Bentley's face as she took her place, but had received a bland, noncommittal smile.

The meeting was called to order by the chairman of the board.

"As all of you know, Dr. Sampson's contract expires the end of the month. We regret his decision to leave us, but that is his choice. I'm happy to announce that we have secured a replacement, a young doctor who will come to us at the completion of his residency. However, we have granted him a month's grace. He will report for duty the first of October." He smiled at Tracy. "Our competent nurse practitioner can carry on very well alone for that period of time."

Cliff looked sharply at Tracy. "But Tracy's leaving with me!"

"We have not yet received her resignation,"

Mrs. Bentley said. "In fact, Tracy told me she has no desire to leave Centerville."

"I know, but her house burned down! I see that as an omen for her to leave. It's time for both of us to seek more gainful employment."

"Money isn't the motivating factor for everyone, Dr. Sampson. It's true that Tracy and I have not always agreed on minor matters. However, time has proven that she was right. I, for one, will exert every effort to keep Tracy with us."

Tracy's expression changed from dazed amazement to tearful joy. All her work—the long hours, the numerous meetings, the patients she had seen—hadn't been in vain. She was appreciated and wanted here in Centerville!

"In fact," Mrs. Bentley continued, "we're taking practical steps to keep Tracy here with us." The other board members all nodded in agreement. "The community has voted to have a house-raising to help rebuild her house."

Tracy's mouth flew open as she gazed in disbelief at one smiling face after another. A house-raising! They would do this for her? Tears flooded her eyes as she reached her hand out to Mrs. Bentley.

"Oh, thank you! Just being wanted means everything. You don't have to help me rebuild."

"But, my dear, we want to! It won't be a mansion, but some of the pre-cut homes are quite nice. Doing this is one way we can show our appreciation."

Aware of Cliff's lowering gaze, Tracy had difficulty keeping her mind on the business being discussed during the rest of the meeting. Now Cliff would have to accept her decision to remain in Centerville. That decision, as she had feared, had been irrevocably settled by Mrs. Bentley. But how differently from what she had envisioned! How she had wronged Mrs. Bentley. Now that she was remaining in Centerville, she would have ample time to right that wrong.

Cliff left as soon as the meeting was dismissed. Tracy would have followed, but a couple of the board members detained her to discuss plans for the house-raising. Could she get the area cleared and decide on plans before October? If they could get the outside framed before the rains started, the inside could be completed at leisure.

Tracy couldn't wait to get home and tell Hattie the exciting news.

"I'm sure Ken can be of help in getting financing," Hattie told her after hugging and kissing her in delight. "Have you decided on house plans yet?"

"Frankly, no. I haven't really done much looking. I've drifted, wondering whether to stay here or go with Cliff to San Mateo."

"Would you have gotten married?"

"Eventually, I suppose. When you've worked as closely as Cliff and I have the past four years, it's hard to think of working with someone new."

"Yes, I can understand that. Still—" Hattie closed her lips on what she was going to say.

Tracy smiled wryly at her. "You were going to mention Andy, weren't you?"

"Yes—even though it's none of my business. Ken says too many women are interested in him, and that he'll never settle into marriage. I've watched him. I think he's in love with you."

Tracy kept her face and voice noncommittal. "Right now the only really important thing in Andy's life is his helicopter business. Love comes second."

The following week passed in a glow of happiness for Tracy. She secured plans from a company which pre-cut redwood lumber to fit various house plans that they sold as a kit.

Tracy pored over the plans, finding it hard to make a decision. In the evening Ken and Hattie pored over the plans with her, offering advice. She was still trying to make up her mind on Friday when Andy came to take her out to dinner. Since Kingsley was sweltering in a heat wave, Andy wanted to drive to the coast. He said little as Tracy told him about the community offer to help her rebuild. However, when they were seated at a restaurant and served iced tea, he raised his glass in a toast.

"To Tracy Nichols, nurse practitioner! And to the community of Centerville for recognizing a rare jewel in their midst. I'm happy for you, my love."

"Not any happier than I am! Aren't people great?"

"Well, I'd have to qualify that. Some people are great. When does this house-raising take place?"

"As soon as I can decide which house I want." She took a manila envelope from beneath her purse. "I just happened to bring the plans along. Would you like to look at them?"

Chuckling, Andy said, "As if I'd dare refuse!" A shadow darkened his face. "My love, this should be our house. If only I could share the building with you instead of it being a community project. Right now—" He shook his head. "There's no way."

Andy liked the largest house, a two-story redwood with solar windows and a sunroom.

"You'd have room to raise a family in this house. And it would fit nicely on your property."

"Dreamer!" Tracy countered. "There's no way I could afford that house. Besides, I have no prospects for a family. One of the other houses will fill my needs nicely."

Tracy finally settled on one of the smaller models with potential for adding on. With the land as collateral, she was able to borrow enough money so that, coupled with the insurance money, she could purchase the kit. In addition, there would be money to cover electrical wiring, plumbing, and kitchen cabinets. Tracy might have to eat off paper plates on a card table and sleep on a cot—so what? She would be under her own roof.

With all of this on her mind, she had completely forgotten her wish to dive for abalone. When Andy phoned to remind her that Saturday promised a full moon and he had borrowed a wet suit for her to wear, she couldn't turn him down. She was up and dressed and had a lunch packed by four A.M. Andy arrived right on time. The morning was chilly, with fog lying on the hills. They drove to the headlands near Mendocino, parked, then climbed down a steep embankment to a rocky cove.

Andy made a fire of driftwood while Tracy changed into her wet suit. He donned one, too. Wearing goggles and fins, they waded to several partly submerged rocks where the water was chest-high. Holding a blunt, curved iron bar, Andy dove below the surface. Soon he surfaced with an abalone. He handed

Tracy the curved iron bar.

"Now you dive and see what you can come up with."

Tracy dove beneath the surface. By the time she saw an abalone adhering to the rock with its muscular foot, she had to come up for air. Laughing, Andy took the iron bar and dove, resurfacing with another catch. Determined not to be outdone, Tracy dove once more, resolving not to surface until she had her abalone.

As though sensing danger, the mollusk clung tenaciously to its rocky perch, resisting her efforts. She pried first on one side, then on the other, holding her breath until she thought her lungs would explode. Just as she decided she had to give up, the abalone came free and fell to the ocean floor. After one futile effort to retrieve it, she had to surface empty-handed and gasping for breath.

"I—I—lost it!"

Andy recovered it and added it to their catch.

Ruefully Tracy said, "I'm not much good at this, am I? It's not like I thought it would be."

"Green Eyes, it's only your first time. Don't be discouraged."

When they had secured their limit and shed their wet suits, they went back to their fire on the beach. Other divers had replenished it and shared the warmth. Tracy

poured hot coffee from a thermos and
unwrapped ham and egg sandwiches, handing one to Andy, keeping the other for herself. All too soon it was time to leave.

Andy stood up first and reached for Tracy's
hand, pulling her to her feet and into his
arms.

"This has been great. Next time you will do
better."

Climbing the embankment to get to the
car, Tracy asked Andy what he planned on
doing with the abalone.

"Clean and freeze them. I'll try to come
once more. Then we'll have an abalone feed
at your house-raising."

Laughing in delight, Tracy said, "If you do
that, everyone in Centerville will be there!"

Pushing steadily ahead, Tracy had the
area cleared and the foundation laid. She was
ready for the big day by the middle of October. On Thursday and Friday the lumber
was trucked in and piled neatly, all labeled
for easy selection. Car after car stopped as
one neighbor after another came by to tell
her they would be at the house-raising on
Saturday.

Her elation and high spirits were damp-
ened by a phone call from her mother.

"Is it true that you're staying in Centerville?" her mother asked. "My dear, I simply

can't understand you giving up that wonderful opportunity to go with Dr. Sampson! At least you would have been back in civilization."

"When my house is completed, you'll have to come for a visit. Then you'll change your mind."

Tracy hung up, unable to shake off the feeling of depression that always followed a call from her mother. Why couldn't her mother understand what her work here meant to her, and how happy she was in the country with her horse and a home of her own? She was brooding over this when Andy phoned.

"Green Eyes, you sound in low spirits. Won't there be a house-raising tomorrow?"

Hearing Andy's voice brought forth a gurgling laugh. "A call from Mom does that to me. Everything's all set for tomorrow — the foundation is in, the building materials have been delivered, and people have been stopping to tell me they will be here in the morning. I'm so excited, I won't be able to sleep."

"Did you get the camp stoves and picnic tables? Fred and Evelyn are coming to help in my culinary project. I hope we have enough abalone."

"Don't worry. The women are all bringing food. There will be plenty to eat."

"What about the beer?" he asked.

"The clinic board of directors are supplying the beer. There'll be wine for lunch. Maurice will bring that. I told him we were having abalone."

"Great! We'll be there around ten."

"Is Sylvia coming?"

"You couldn't keep her away!"

"Oh, Andy! I can't get used to the idea people are doing this for me!"

"My love, you deserve it or they wouldn't be doing it. I just hope all who come are better with a hammer and nails than I am!"

Tracy awoke at the first hint of dawn and looked out her window. What a glorious Indian summer day this was going to be! No fog lay on the hills, and not a single cloud marred the blue expanse of sky. She dressed in jeans and a bright red T-shirt and was eating a dish of cold cereal when Billy joined her. His fractured leg had healed without complication and he was as excited as she was about the house-raising.

"Mom says I'm not to get in the way, but I can help, can't I?" he asked, gulping a glass of milk.

"I'm sure there will be something for everyone to do. You can go over with me now if you want to."

By eight o'clock the workers had arrived,

material had been organized, and the sound of hammering filled the air. A young carpenter acted as supervisor. His two-year-old son had recently swallowed poison and Tracy, by her swift action, had prevented any lasting damage to the child. As she looked around, she realized that every person there had had some member of the family treated at the clinic.

Andy, Sylvia, Fred, and Evelyn arrived a little after ten and, selecting a clearing in a grove of trees, set up their camp kitchen. Several neighbors had responded by bringing folding tables and chairs. Baked beans, green salads, homemade bread, and cakes and pies appeared as if by magic. Tracy had prepared hamburger patties and bought franks, too. She smiled with satisfaction. Andy needn't worry about not having enough food.

Andy and Fred had everything ready before starting the abalone. Andy sauntered over to stand with Tracy and watch the men working on the house.

"Sounds as active as a beehive, doesn't it?" Andy said. A bee buzzed by his ear. "Speaking of bees!" He swatted at the big insect, but missed, then watched it buzzing around Tracy. "Keep that thing away from me! I swell up like a balloon if I get stung!"

He had hardly spoken the words before the bee settled on his bare arm. He let out a howl.

"Andy! Did you get stung?"

Tracy grabbed his arm and saw that the insect had flown away. She gently scraped the stinger to remove it, then hurried Andy to a tap so she could wash his arm.

"Are you allergic to bee stings?" she asked.

"Last time I got stung, I nearly died."

"Then let me get you to the clinic! My car's right here."

As long as she lived, Tracy would remember the drive to the clinic. Andy began to look terrible, and he couldn't breathe. Should she have brought someone with her? she wondered. What if Andy went into shock?

At the clinic she got him to a treatment room. Then she quickly injected him with adrenaline.

He looked better.

"Tracy—love—"

The adrenaline had to work, it had to! Nothing like this could happen to Andy! He couldn't die!

It seemed ages, but in reality it was only minutes until full color returned to Andy's face and his breathing became easy and regular. Unable to stop her tears, Tracy bent down and kissed him.

"My darling."

A sweet, tender smile lit up his face. He raised a trembling hand to brush at a tear on her cheek.

"Green Eyes, love, no tears!"

"Oh, Andy! I was so frightened!"

The old, teasing light sparkled in the brown eyes as he lifted her hand and kissed it.

"You were frightened! I was terrified." He rubbed his throat. "That feeling of suffocation! I knew I was a goner." Eyes somber, hand trembling, he wiped away another tear trickling down Tracy's face. "My green-eyed angel of mercy! My life! Darling, how soon can we be married?"

Tracy stared at him. "But, Andy, your business! Your partnership with Sylvia."

"Hang my business and Sylvia! I love you and want to spend the rest of my life with you."

Face radiant with joy, Tracy smiled her acceptance. "We'll be married as soon as the house is livable."

Andy started to get up from the treatment table. "Then let's get on with it!"

Alarmed, Tracy pushed Andy back down. "Absolutely not. You have to rest several hours. You're staying right here until I say you can get up."

"Not unless you stay with me."

"Well—"

"Get in touch with Fred. He'll handle everything. Just tell him to save two servings of abalone. We'll be there later to join..."

Andy's eyes closed and his voice trailed off to silence. Tracy brushed a stray lock of red hair off his forehead, then brushed each closed eye with her lips. She hated to miss the picnic lunch. The women had all worked so hard. Still, they would understand and forgive her. When the house was completed, she and Andy could invite them back for another abalone feed.

Yes, the house would be completed and Andy would share it with her. What a joyful thought! They would still have to face Sylvia, and it would be a financial struggle. But they would face the future together. No matter how bumpy the road, love would smooth the way.